Courageous

Russ Crossley

Edited by R. Edgewood

Published by 53rd Street Publishing

Offices in Gibsons, B.C. Canada and Lincoln City, Oregon

Other collections and anthologies from the author

In an alternate reality the Confederate States won the civil war because they had a deadly supernatural ally. Only she could stop them...

The side cargo door swung upward on hydraulic arms accompanied by the soft whir of the motors. Immediately two armed CSA police troopers burst out onto the squashed grass, dressed in head to foot gray and green battle armor, the faceplates closed, their automags scanning the area around them ready to fire on anyone foolish enough to attack.

From bitter experience, Amy knew the troopers' weapons were loaded with rounds that would shred her into fleshy ribbons of bloody meat that even her ability to heal would be useless against. The CSA had learned the most efficient method to destroy a vampire without holy water or wooden stakes. Those ancient weapons against the undead were a thing of the past. Why risk close and personal? Why not kill from a safe distance?

Acknowledgments

Thank you to our editor, Colleen Kuehne, for her diligent work to improve our work. We are forever grateful to her. And to all those authors who inspired the book you have in your hands. Thank you all for your wonderful stories involving women of strength.

Dedication

For Rita who shares my love of the fantastic.

Courageous

Russ Crossley

Edited by R. Edgewood

Published by 53rd Street Publishing

Cover art © Eti Swinford | Dreamstime.com
Cover designed by R. Edgewood
Cover design and layout © 2015 by 53rd Street
Publishing

Print ISBN: 978-1-927621-46-2
53rd Street Publishing
Head office: Gibsons B.C. Canada
www.53rdstreetpublishing.com

This is a work of fiction. Any similarities to persons living or dead are purely coincidental.

Table of Contents

Introduction

About the Author

Other titles available from 53rd Street Publishing

Introduction

I have been a fan of women in science fiction and fantasy since I began reading. The stories that inspire me are the ones where courage is tested and the heroines must rise to overcome seemingly impossible odds. Reading pulse pounding tales like these left me awestruck.

These selected tales offer the same sense of awe and wonder that thrilled me all those years ago and I hope will do the same for you.

Enjoy!

R. Edgewood

September 2015

Ghost stories have long been one of my favorite subgenres of the horror genre. This tale involves a young woman gone before her time and the woman she turns to for help, Amanda Dark, Paranormal Investigator.

A Father's Daughter

SAFFRON SHIFTED HER BOTTOM ON THE HARD PINE CHAIR, where she sat studying the unadorned steel-gray walls and floor of the ten-by-ten-foot room surrounding the burnished steel desk in the center of the otherwise bare room. Looking down at herself, she discovered she was dressed in black slacks, flats, and a white cotton long-sleeved shirt. The clothes reminded her of the K-Mart housewives she silently mocked when she made trips to the mall to visit the high-end shops for new shoes and the latest fashions. She had closets reserved just for her shoes. She had never worn such frumpy clothes in her life.

Seated across from her in a brown, well-worn leather chair, was a pale-faced, severe-looking woman with mint green eyes, her angular features focused on the pages of a large, clothbound book, open on the desk in front of her.

Saffron had no sense of how long she'd been here or how she'd gotten here. But she did have a vague sense of unease, deep in her belly, that had formed a knot reminiscent of hunger.

Yet she wasn't hungry, at least not exactly, as she thought of hunger. In the recesses of her mind, memories bubbled of the taste of champagne and cherries and coffee, but she had no compulsion or need for them. Something had changed. But what?

Saffron's auburn eyes finally landed on the woman across from her, who smelled of peppermints and chamomile tea like her grandmother, who had died when she and her twin sister, Sadie, were fifteen years old. Their father had taken them with him to retrieve her grandmother's clothes for the funeral. She recalled seeing the hairbrush lying face up on her grandmother's antique mirrored dresser, the battleship-gray wisps of hair still clinging to the stiff, black horsehair bristles as if trapped for eternity as the only remaining evidence of the woman who gave her chocolate candies at Christmas, and sent crisp, new dollar bills for her and her sister in a birthday card each year.

A twinge of regret for the unkindness toward her elderly grandmother invaded her thoughts briefly, then retreated immediately. As long as she could recall, her grandmother had been trapped in a frail body twisted by painful arthritis. Saffron had been young and stupid then, a horribly self-absorbed teenager who failed to appreciate her elders.

Her deepest regret was reserved for her father, whose angry eyes bore into her when, at her grandmother's funeral, she and her sister had giggled at some inane private joke between them.

Mercifully he never spoke to her about the incident, but she knew they had disappointed him. Her beloved father was the only man she had ever looked to for wisdom and guidance. Most of the men she dated were spoiled pretty-boys with more money than brains. They definitely weren't the type of men she would ever marry or turn to for advice.

She had always wanted to apologize to her father for her behavior, but had never had the courage to bring up the subject with him. Since that day, she'd considered their relationship irrecoverably damaged.

Looking around the bare room, she somehow sensed that her opportunity to tell her father how she felt had passed.

"Miss Smythe?" said the woman, startling her from her moment of retrospection. The woman's voice had a deep timber and an edge of disapproval. Hanging from her neck by a thin chain was a pair of horn-rimmed glasses. She was wearing a dowdy dress of navy-blue roses over a pale beige background. A button at the neck secured the collar. Her dark hair was shot through with gray streaks and was tied into a bun atop her narrow head.

"Yes. Saffron Smythe, actually."

One pepper-colored eyebrow arched on her pale forehead as she regarded Saffron, obviously unimpressed. "Yes," she said, "Saffron, of course." The woman interlaced her long, tapered fingers on top of the pages of the open book, then leaned slightly forward, her elbows resting on the book. Her dispassionate gaze made Saffron uncomfortable. "According to our records, you are here slightly earlier than expected."

"Ummmm, that's the thing, Ms...." Saffron looked at the woman questioningly.

"Ruth. You may call me Ruth." A slight hitch in Ruth's tone suggested Saffron was to continue.

She had a small, humorless smile on her lips.

Saffron nodded. "I'm not sure where I am, exactly."

The woman nodded, unlaced her fingers, and eased back in her chair, her expression sending Saffron signals that she had heard this question many times. "Of course. Many who arrive here have no idea their existence on Earth is at an end."

Saffron froze and her jaw dropped. She shivered as if she was suddenly chilled, except the room's temperature was nearly perfect. "Do you mean I'm dead?"

A sardonic smile spread across Ruth's features. "Yes. But don't be concerned. You're in the best of hands. I'll soon have your next assignment ready."

"But I can't be dead," Saffron whispered. "I'm too young. And I'm too rich."

Ruth grinned. "I hear that *a lot,* more often than you might think, actually."

Anger bubbled up from Saffron's stomach. She tasted sour bile at the back of her throat. *How can I be dead and still taste bile*? She sucked in a breath, then exhaled. *I seem to be breathing.* She pinched the skin of her right arm between thumb and forefinger as hard as she could, and winced at the sudden rush of pain.

Son of a bi— She spat her next words between gritted teeth. "Lady, I don't know who you are, but I'm the daughter of a very powerful man, so I suggest you let me go immediately."

"Oh, but Saffron, no one is holding you here, I assure you. This is a way station. My job is to prepare you for your final destination."

Saffron's anger subsided and she eyed the woman. "Final destination?" She had a bad feeling about Ruth's answer. She knew somehow she wouldn't like it.

A sardonic grin came over Ruth's pale features and her eyes narrowed. "Yes," Ruth said simply, offering no further explanation.

Saffron tried to recall where she had been and what she had been doing before realizing she was in this windowless room across a desk from this woman who reeked of peppermints. No matter how she tried, it was as if her mind was in a fog.

"It's okay, Saffron. It's unlikely you'll be able to recall anything from the time before you died except for flashes of stray thoughts that may seem like dreams. But don't be concerned. This is often taxing on new arrivals at first, but with time, you will understand.

Most new arrivals find that when they are allowed into the hall of memories, they begin to comprehend what they had been in life and what they are now." Ruth spoke as if these cryptic words made perfect sense; however, Saffron remained thoroughly confused.

This lady is nutso. "Okay, I get it, I'm dead and this is heaven...but how did I die?" Saffron suddenly froze when an image formed of herself lying in a bathtub, buried in an ocean of white foam. She was somehow hovering over herself, looking down at her naked form through the dissipating bubbles, lying on her back under the water in the marble tub. Her body was limp, unmoving, her eyes closed. Saffron realized the *her* in the bathtub wasn't breathing and the lips were pale, the skin on the face a sickly gray pallor. A half empty crystal champagne flute sat on the edge of the tub. The bubbles in the wine having long ago dispersed meant the flute had sat untouched for too long and gone flat.

It dawned on her she had died while having a bubble bath.

She loved bubble baths, the water lapping against her skin like a silk blanket, the warm steam rising from the white jasmine-scented bubbles. Surely she wasn't meant to die in a bath?

Saffron licked her lips. *I loved the taste of champagne on my tongue.*

Ruth laughed lightly, causing the corners of her eyes to crinkle. "No, this isn't heaven. As I said before, this is a way station where you will receive your next assignment."

Saffron studied the woman's placid features, then her eyes dropped to look at the book. "What's in the book?" she asked.

"This is a record of each person's date of death. My job is to fill in the column listing each arrival's final destination—once I'm told, of course."

Saffron's eyes narrowed. "Told? Told by whom?"

Suddenly a telephone began to emit a muffled ring. Ruth smiled and reached down to open a drawer in the desk beside her. She withdrew a telephone as black as licorice, with a heavy black wire trailing off the back of the unit and a dial face on the front, covering a white background depicting large numbers and small block letters under each opening in the dial. There was a receiver in a cradle on the top, attached the main body by a wire. As Ruth set it on the desk with a soft *thump*, it rang again, only louder this time since the drawer didn't muffle it.

Saffron had never seen a telephone like it. Where was Ruth's cell phone?

Ruth picked up the receiver and held it to her ear. "Yes?" She listened intently to whomever had called, her expression changing from pleased, to concern, to puzzlement. Finally she said good-bye and hung up. Her eyes reflected her astonishment.

She sighed before she spoke. "This happens so rarely I am surprised every time it does." Ruth paused, adding to Saffron's discomfort. Finally she continued. "I'm advised you are to be sent back to Earth."

She paused again to look into Saffron's eyes since they must have revealed her excitement.

I'm going home.

"I'm sorry, I'm not being clear. Your spirit will be sent to Earth, but your interaction with living beings will be quite limited." Ruth cleared her throat, Saffron sensing the woman's hesitation. "It appears you have indeed arrived earlier than expected because you were murdered."

Oh, shit. I'm in trouble. I need Amanda Dark.

***

Saffron had no sense of movement but she suddenly materialized in Phillip Swann's office, one of many in the law offices of Smythe, Wellington, Goldberg, and Thompson.

Her senses were immediately assaulted by the scent of wood polish, which wasn't surprising as the Boston law firm had never removed the original teak paneling since the prestigious firm opened in 1902. Such expensive wood required constant care to maintain its gleaming, pristine appearance, but the partners agreed it added to the firm's elegant image. The firm had represented Boston's social elite worldwide for over a hundred years. Of course, she knew this because her great-great-great-grandfather had been the founder and an original partner of the firm. Her father still represented the family name on the masthead.

Before the way station disappeared as if in a fog, Ruth explained Saffron had been granted one visit outside the place she was to haunt until the matter of her murder was settled. By settled, of course, Ruth meant the murder was solved and the killer brought to justice. Only then would Saffron return to the way station to be assigned her final destination.

She would be able to interact with one living person and be able to experience sensory details of the environment around her since this might help trigger memories essential to solving the crime. Ruth ended by warning her it might take some time, so she must be patient.

As if looking through a veil of mist, Saffron saw Phillip Swann come into focus. He was seated in a black leather executive chair behind a massive, fifty-year-old teak desk, examining documents one by one from a thick file. The wood of the desk was stained dark and polished to a gleaming shine under the light of the crystal chandelier in the ten-foot-high ceiling overhead. A silver executive telephone was to Phillip's right and a large, flat computer screen was to his left. Behind his desk and running the length of the long office wall were built-in bookcases containing volumes of law books. One wall was a floor-to-ceiling picture window overlooking the bustling city streets far below. The glass was tinted so it wasn't too bright in the offices, even on the sunniest of days.

But Saffron's attention was drawn to Amanda Dark, who was seated in a horseshoe-shaped leather chair, watching Phillip from the other side of his massive desk. Amanda was a short woman, just over five feet in height; of medium build, not buxom and not thin; with mouse-brown hair cut to brush her shoulders. Her pleasant features, wide set curious hazel eyes, and smallish nose meant she couldn't be described as beautiful, but she wasn't ugly, either. Right now Amanda's eyes gazed at Phillip with a look in them Saffron knew well.

The woman loved the firm's associate more than she was willing to admit.

With his jet-black, curly hair cut military short, his square jaw, and dimples in both cheeks when he smiled, Saffron well understood Phillip's appeal. His narrow waist and lightly muscled arms under his tailored suits and shirts told her he took care of his appearance, but then, any lawyer whose goal was to become a partner needed every weapon in his arsenal to get there. Phillip Swann was bright, personable, and good looking, so he'd surely make partner someday.

Saffron had met Phillip and Amanda at one of her father's mixers held in the office a couple of times a year. Normally she avoided such stuffy affairs, preferring to hit the many clubs and bars around Boston with peers her own age; but for some reason, that day she attended the party where she met the young, handsome associate and his unlikely wannabe girlfriend.

Amanda claimed to be a paranormal detective. She hadn't explained what the job entailed, but Saffron soon learned that the plain-speaking woman had helped Phillip on a number of difficult estate cases resulting in very grateful and very wealthy clients who paid considerable sums to the firm.

Once, after a few too many drinks, her father told her Amanda Dark was a ghost whisperer and that she could speak to the spirits of the dead. Saffron thought this nonsense; she didn't believe in ghosts.

But when Ruth asked who she would like to see on Earth, Saffron immediately asked for Amanda Dark. Even if she were a fake, she had helped some big cases for the firm so she had to have some talent for dealing with the paranormal—or she was the most successful grifter in history. Seeing Amanda's K-Mart wardrobe of gray cotton slacks, white, no-name brand runners, and sleeveless, mint-green rayon top didn't scream flourishing con artist. Saffron doubted the latter was true.

Suddenly Saffron froze as Amanda visibly stiffened. She was looking right at her, her eyes growing wide—not with fear but with surprise. *She sees me now.*

"Uh, Phil, we have a visitor," Amanda said in a low voice.

"Ummm," said Phillip, his attention focused on a document he was reading from the file folder. "Tell them I'm busy."

"It's not *that* kind of visitor," explained Amanda, her voice louder now.

Phillip stopped reading as his brow wrinkled and he looked up at Amanda. "A ghost?" he asked as if it were an every day occurrence. In fact, Saffron could swear his expression was one of annoyance. "In my office?" He shook his head. "No way. We've never had a ghost in my office. You must be mistaken."

Amanda shook her head, her eyes still locked on Saffron, who stood still with a tight grin on her lips. "In fact, I think it's Robert Smythe's daughter."

Phillip grunted. "Really? Which one?" He scanned the room. "I don't see anyone."

Amanda grunted, then turned her head to scowl at him as if he were a small child. "Really, Phil, do we have to go through this *again*?"

Phillip's shoulders relaxed and he grinned, the dimples in his cheeks deepening. "I'm kidding, Amanda. Surely by now you know when I'm joking?"

The tension in Amanda's body eased and she chuckled. "Sorry, Phil, but you know how I am about my work."

"Amanda," interrupted Saffron, "have you two finished your mating dance yet? I have a big problem I need your help with."

Amanda shifted her attention to Saffron. "Sorry, Ms. Smythe, Phil and I are so used to ghosts and we too often verbally spar in front of them."

Her hazel eyes flitted to a grinning Phillip Swann, who eased back in his chair while maintaining his silence, then back to her. "What can I do for you?"

These two seemed to be laughing at her. *I've been murdered, for God's sake.*

A knot of anger formed in her stomach. Old habits from her impetuous, over-privileged youth were going to be tougher to break than she thought. She could not deny in life she had been a rich, spoiled brat, but now that she was dead, she had vowed to be better in the afterlife.

She managed to push the anger away before she spoke. "Please call me Saffron. Ms. Smythe was my late mother, God rest her soul." She paused as the humor faded from Amanda's eyes. Saffron then blurted, "I've been murdered. I desperately need your help to catch the killer."

***

Saffron stood on the cold marble floor of the expansive foyer of Smythe Hall, Amanda beside her. The sweeping circular staircase curled up and into the distance to the upper floors of the ten-bedroom, ten-bathroom mansion.

The floor-to-ceiling crushed-red-velvet drapes over the tall windows bordering the cool foyer were drawn shut, requiring the large crystal chandelier hanging twenty-five feet above their heads to be illuminated, even though it was early afternoon on a summer day. The musty air spoke of age and neglect. Saffron realized something had happened in her family home—something bad.

Amanda coughed to clear her throat. "Phil said your father agreed to meet me...I mean us."

"You didn't tell him about me, did you?"

Amanda shook her head. "If I did, do you think he would agree to see me?"

Saffron sighed. Of course Amanda was correct. If she told him she had spoken to his dead daughter, he'd have dismissed her as a kook after his money. Her father was a practical man if nothing else.

"I have a question."

Amanda looked at her with a curious expression. Saffron continued. "How can I be dead so long but only now become..." Her words trailed off. She couldn't say the word ghost it sounded ridiculous.

How long ago did I die? For the first time, it occurred to her to wonder how long she'd been dead.

"When did I die?"

Amanda's brow wrinkled. "Space and time are very different in the after life. Time isn't linear—"

She was about to explain more when somewhere overhead a generator suddenly whirred to life in the silent, dusty air that stank of stale coffee and burnt toast interrupting them. Amanda eyes suggested that later might be a better time to talk.

Reluctantly Saffron agreed. She had a sense time was short, even though in reality she had more time now than she'd ever had in life.

Saffron saw a slit of light coming from the bottom of a closet door on the left side of the foyer that, as she recalled, contained her mother's and father's long evening coats.

The slit of light grew brighter as a rumbling sound and the whine of the generator increased in intensity. Finally there was a deep *thud* and the door of the closet slid aside to reveal a wizened man with white hair in a wheelchair. His gray eyes studied Amanda, his pale brow wrinkled by curiosity.

Saffron sucked in a breath as the man's long fingers worked a control stick on the right armrest of the wheelchair and it rolled out of the closet, now obviously converted to an elevator, onto the marble floor.

Tears blurred her vision as she realized the man was her father.

The once vital, healthy man who drank protein shakes for breakfast, ran in marathons, and worked out at the firm's gym three times a week had been replaced by these fossil-like remains.

Amanda's features were lit by a smile as she stepped forward to greet her father in the wheelchair. He appeared worn and tired, his once alert, steady gaze dull and lifeless as if he'd lost hope. His features were gaunt, his cheeks sunken, his skin had a gray pallor.

Upon fully seeing his appearance, Saffron's heart ached for her father as her eyes welled with tears. Ruth promised she'd experience everything she saw, heard, and smelled—complete with the accompanying emotional reactions—as if she were still alive. But she'd be unable to offer comfort to those who needed it or speak with anyone other than Amanda.

If I'd only known my father needed me so badly, I would have asked to speak with him instead of Amanda. She may not have been able to solve her murder, but her father needed her and that was more important right now.

Amanda stuck out one hand, which her father ignored, preferring to keep his hands folded in his lap. He was dressed in a navy-blue tracksuit, his feet covered by slippers that were almost worn through with use. The front of the zippered jacket was covered in soup stains. "Mr. Smythe, it's a pleasure to see you again, sir. How long has it been? Ten years?"

His eyes narrowed. "Do I know you?" he asked, his voice raspy and dry.

Amanda dropped her hand to her side, her smile still bright and inviting. "I'm Amanda Dark. Phillip Swann's friend."

His brow creased in thought for several seconds until he nodded. "Yes, the ghost person. You talk to the dead."

"Yes, sir, I am blessed, or some would say cursed, with that particular gift."

The old man eyed her with one gray eyebrow arched. "My daughter died eight years ago. Are you communicating with her ghost now, is that why you're here?" He snorted bitterly. "And I suppose you want money."

Amanda shook her head. "No, sir, Phillip works for you at the firm and your daughter approached us asking for our help. We won't be billing anything for my services."

Robert Swann shook his head. "She died in a car accident. Why would she want to talk to me now, after all this time?"

Car accident? thought Saffron. "Amanda, who died in a car accident? I drowned in a bathtub. I remember it."

Amanda nodded to Saffron. "Sir, I thought your daughter drowned."

Robert laughed derisively, his humor tainted with bitterness. "No, no, that's Saffron. That lazy, ungrateful drunk drowned herself after partying all night with her so-called friends. She spent my money recklessly and selfishly. She deserved to die." He paused and hung his head.

"My precious Sadie, she died in the car wreck not a mile from the estate. Her death ended my life's work." A tear escaped his right eye, running down his cheek until it fell off the edge of his bony chin to splash on the foyer floor.

Saffron couldn't believe what she was hearing. If she had been murdered, then either her father had done it or her beloved twin sister had done the deed. She suspected she'd been drugged, then passed out in the bathtub and drowned. An engineered accident covered up by a powerful law firm with friends in high places, including the police department.

"Amanda," Saffron whispered. "Don't go any further. I don't want to know."

Amanda looked at her with wide eyes. "But it means you won't be able to go to your final destination, ever."

"Are you crazy, woman?" asked Robert, his eyes wild and his cheeks flushed by a surge of anger. "Who are you talking to?"

Amanda turned to face Robert in his wheelchair. "Your daughter, Saffron, is here with me," she said, glaring at him. "And right now, I must explain a few things to her; then you and I must talk. Sir," she added firmly, her hazel eyes now hard, the smile but a memory.

Robert sagged in his chair, his hands fidgeting erratically in his lap, his face twisted by a scowl.

Amanda faced Saffron. "I checked your file at Phillip's office before I came here." She paused and Saffron could see the mix of emotions on her wholesome features. The paranormal detective took in a deep breath to steady herself and then continued. "Yes, you died in the bath. Drowned, as you say. The police investigated after the coroner determined you had an overdose of sleeping pills in your blood stream.

"The investigation resulted in a ruling of accidental overdose, which led to your drowning. Then there was a notation found in your diary—"

"Sadie wrote the suicide note in Saffron's diary," Robert suddenly blurted, his words angry. "I provided the overdose of pills. I killed my own daughter." He steered the wheelchair across the marble floor, right at Amanda, who stepped aside as he stopped. He stuck out a bony index finger at her. "And I'd do it again. Sadie deserved a chance to run the firm. She was a lawyer but their late mother, who controlled the real family money, included a clause in her will that required the firm be sold after my death and the proceeds divided equally between the twins.

"Sadie would have saved *my* firm from extinction. Saffron was a party girl who would have destroyed the firm I built. All she cared about was satisfying her own selfish pleasures. If anything happened to Sadie after I died Saffron would have assumed control of the firm." He sagged in his chair and his voice dropped to a hoarse whisper. "I couldn't le that happen."

"Sadie would have kept up the family tradition. Saffron deserved to die so her sister could inherit the business." He paused when his voice cracked.

Clearing his throat Robert shook his head. "It seemed to make sense then...now that my own days are numbered I'm not so sure."

His watery gaze shifted to Amanda. "I realize now I was wrong. Tell Saffron I'm sorry. I made a mistake." He began to sob, and Saffron sensed his terrible pain and regret.

Amanda looked again at Saffron. "Well, what do you want to do?"

Saffron thought for a few seconds and then made up her mind. "I'm going to stay at Smythe Hall by my father's side until he dies. I still love him and I forgive him."

"You do know you won't be able to change your mind?"

Saffron nodded.

The doorbell rang, interrupting them. Amanda went to the door and pulled the drape aside. Phillip stood at the door. She waved to him, then turned back to face Robert Smythe, who gazed back at her with red-rimmed eyes.

"Mr. Smythe, I'm going to leave you now. I wish you well, sir, but I still feel your daughter has made a poor decision. If I had my way, and there were sufficient evidence, I would go to the police.

"But I imagine the extensive cover-up of your crime and the fact it occurred ten years ago make any investigation not worthwhile."

Ignoring Amanda's words, Robert Smythe's eyes reflect his realization that his murdered daughter's spirit was in the room with them. "What did Saffron decide?"

"She's forgiven you and will be staying on as the resident ghost of Smythe Hall." The corners of Amanda's mouth curled up slightly as she shared a knowing look with Saffron. "At least for a while."

Amanda then opened the front door and went outside, closing it with a soft *thump* behind her.

Saffron gazed at her father in his wheelchair, his pale gray eyes fearful, and wondered how long he would live. She would haunt him until then, hopefully helping him to come to grips with what he had done and the consequences he might suffer when his day at the way station came. She wondered where Ruth would assign him. *Probably not the place with the wings.*

One thing she knew for certain; she would see Amanda Dark again, when the time was right.

Since the creation of the planet human beings have always wondered how the world will end. There are countless stories across all media formats speculating about the apocalypse. This tale tells the story of a group of people who refuse to go into the night with a whimper.

Neighborhood Watch

THE FLICKERING FLAME FROM THE OIL LAMP cast twisted, writhing shadows over the walls of Pete Simpson's recreation room in the basement of his split-level, four-bedroom house. The large room was a real man cave. Even after all this time, the room still smelled of cigar smoke and beer, though we hadn't had either of those luxuries since this all began six weeks ago. We four neighborhood watch members were seated around a seven-player mahogany poker table.

The playing surface was covered in a tobacco-colored leather, with integrated chip wells and cup holders.

We were waiting for the arrival of the fifth member of our group. Seven armless, matching leather chairs surrounded the table.

Only we weren't here to play poker.

Along the walls of the oblong-shaped room were burnished steel shelves containing trophies and plaques from Pete's days as a high school and state collegiate athlete. Amongst these personal treasures were his sports collectibles signed baseballs, basketballs, and footballs representing every pro team in the state of Washington and in Portland, Oregon, just across the Columbia River.

In a wide gap in the bookshelves was a sixty-inch flat screen television. Facing the large digital TV were two rows of leather recliners, five chairs in each row. The simulated oak flooring stood up to the punishment of Sunday NFL games and final four weekends.

Pete hadn't been a star amongst his athletic peers but he had been pretty good. Too bad for him, others were better. They received the scholarships while Pete became a used car salesman who lived in our middle class neighborhood on the outskirts of Vancouver. He was trapped in suburbia along with the rest of us.

Of course, his collectibles and trophies were worthless now.

No one is going to barter for a can of tuna with a collectible anymore, not when cash money, gold, and diamonds have no value. Especially when you and your family will starve to death without food. Food and water meant survival. How ironic it was that we'd wasted our lives striving for now worthless stuff.

"Where's Oscar?" asked Alice, who was seated across from me, her dark eyes narrowed to slits. She was constantly wringing her hands as if washing them. Her short brown hair was oily and she reeked of sour sweat, but then, didn't we all? None of us had had enough water to shower or bathe for weeks now. We'd thought about going to the river, but being outside our barricaded neighborhood was risky and presented serious security issues for us.

My poor friend, Alice, was nervous and becoming increasingly edgy over the past few days. Recent events had brought us all to the edge of our sanity.

The lacquered pine paneling that lined the walls behind the shelves had always bothered me. Who in their right mind would keep this cheap '60s crap on their walls? I rolled my eyes since I knew the answer without asking the question. A Neanderthal like Pete, seated to my right, of course.

With his thinning hair and receding hairline and expanding beer gut, he had become the poster boy around the neighborhood for the fading athlete. Now, of course, he was a shriveled man—half his former size, with sunken, grizzled cheeks.

"Got the time?" I asked Conrad, seated across the table from me. He looked at his mechanical watch and his lips formed a grim, humorless line. "He's more than an hour overdue."

I slapped Pete's left shoulder with the back of my hand. "I thought you said he'd be back with the scouting party by now?"

Pete scowled at me, his piercing cobalt eyes angry. "Knock it off, Liz, I'm as worried about them as you are. We all know the risks."

"Yeah," I said, sweeping stray lengths of my scraggly, dirty-blonde hair away from over my eyes with my arm. I hadn't had a decent haircut in weeks and had decided earlier today to shave my head completely as many of the neighborhood women and some men had done, although I loved my long hair. It had taken years to grow it this long.

"But they promised us we had ninety days," said May. "Surely we can last at least that long."

May was Chinese-American, with dark, almond-shaped eyes that seemed to look right through you, and high cheekbones. She'd always been thin but now her bare arms looked skeletal in her sleeveless, pink, cotton top.

I gritted my teeth as my guts twisted. May's words tore through me like a knife, but I knew she was right. The voluntary ration system wasn't working. Individual greed had overcome the greater good. We were failing. The truth, I knew, was not greed but survival, a very human instinct in these circumstances. People in the neighborhood had been hoarding supplies for themselves, not sharing as we had all agreed.

At the neighborhood watch meeting convened a week after they arrived and cut off the power, representatives from every house in our subdivision agreed to work for the common good. Now that supplies were becoming scarce, it was becoming obvious not everyone was sharing everything.

If Oscar and his small force of four men and two women didn't return from the latest mission, it was bad news for the neighborhood. Several times, food- and medicine-scrounging missions had disappeared in the past two weeks.

These volunteers were sent out heavily armed, with guns collected from the neighborhood residents for a collective armory. Their unexplained disappearance meant conditions outside the barricades we'd set up after the power grid failed were getting worse, or something too terrible to contemplate was happening. Our role as neighborhood leaders may have also broken down. I wished now Oscar hadn't agreed to lead this last mission himself, but he had explained that we as leaders needed to lead and show the people we accepted the same risks as everyone else.

Before he left, he told me privately he'd determine what had happened to the other teams if he could.

If our leadership failed to maintain control, then we'd fall into anarchy, survival of the fittest would surpass all other considerations, and we'd have a crisis on our hands. The thought of quelling an uprising of my friends and neighbors caused me many sleepless nights.

A few of the neighborhood men were former military, or reservists like Pete, who had skills with weapons.

Many of these qualified former soldiers were manning the makeshift barricades, composed of trucks and cars that had been abandoned after the fuel supply was gone and various pieces of furniture, surrounding the perimeter of the ten block radius we were responsible for. So far, our internal communications system had been working.

We'd been using old analog, battery-operated walkie-talkies, but the supply of batteries, as with the food and water, was nearly exhausted.

Our neighborhood consisted of fifty homes originally containing two hundred and twenty-five residents. In the past six weeks, we'd lost thirty-five in total. Fifteen disappeared on supply missions, an equal number of the elderly and the very young were lost to starvation, suicides made up the balance of our losses. We were down to one hundred ninety warm bodies. Many were physically capable but I wasn't so sure about many of these peoples mental state.

Suddenly we heard footsteps pounding down the stairs from above us and Sue Burns burst into to the room, her breath coming in gasps, her lean arms and bare legs covered in a sheen of sweat. Her tan shorts and white top were sweat stained and greasy. Her green eyes were wild and unfocused by fear.

In her trembling right hand she held a walkie-talkie. In her left was the AR-15 semi-auto rifle I had given her after she completed firearms training two weeks ago.

"Sue," I said in a voice meant to calm her. "Calm down."

Sue nodded but her eyes flitted between the assembled leaders still seated at the table and she was avoiding making eye contact with me. Her breathing steadied but her worn Nikes still shifted side to side. The woman was as jumpy as a cat on summer-heated blacktop.

I stood, then placed my hands on the sides of her narrow shoulders to steady her and stared into her eyes. "What's wrong, Sue?"

She finally looked at me, but her eyes were placid and eerily free of any emotion I could recognize. It was as if she was now at the center of a hurricane. "Uhhhh...there's a group of armed people approaching the north side of the barricades near Elmont Street," she said, her voice a dry hoarse whisper.

My breath caught in my throat. I looked over my shoulder at Pete, who had visibly tensed. "You and the others go ahead and check it out. I'll be along shortly."

Pete's tanned brow wrinkled and his eyes narrowed. He stood and signaled to the others to stand, too, then nodded. He hurried up the stairs with May and Alice close behind. I heard the echo of their footsteps thump up the stairs until there again was silence. Before they left the house, they would arm themselves and then head for the Elmont Street barricade.

I directed my attention to studying Sue's sweaty features. Her shoulders sagged and I knew the adrenaline driving her was ebbing. I gently took the walkie-talkie from her and set it on the poker table. I then slipped my fingers around the barrel of the rifle gripped in her left hand, intending to take it from her as well.

Sue's normally placid, oval-shaped face shifted to anger, her eyes glaring at me. I sensed the strength returning to her lean frame. She pulled the gun away violently, forcing me to reluctantly release the weapon. In her present state, Sue was probably dangerous to herself and others.

This was confirmed when I saw the look in her eyes and knew she had lost touch with reality. For the first time since the beginning of the crisis, it occurred to me that a neighbor might shoot me. "Sue, tell me what's wrong."

I spoke in an even tone so as not to spook her.

"I need the gun," she said between gritted teeth. I stepped back and gave her room, raising my hands in surrender.

"Why don't you sit and we'll talk?"

Sue's eyes narrowed and a bead of sweat ran down her sunburned cheek. "You're trying to trick me. You want my gun." She pointed the muzzle at me, her right index finger hovering over the trigger. "I will kill you...anyone...who tries to take my gun." Her voice was low and threatening.

I smiled and sat down, placing my hands, one over the other, on the table and resting my weight on my forearms. "No, of course I won't take your gun. If you recall, I was the one who gave it to you." I kept my tone light.

Sue's features twisted in confusion, anger, and suspicion all at once. I'd succeeded in confusing her. Slowly she lowered the gun and dropped into the chair across from me, the AR-15 hanging loose at her side, the barrel pointed at the floor. She appeared exhausted, the last of her inner resources spent. A sense of relief washed over me.

I walked around the table until I stood beside her slumping body. Her eyelids were heavy with sleep.

I carefully reached for the rifle and managed to gingerly release her now loose grip when she suddenly bolted upright, grabbing for the barrel. I pulled hard and wrested it away from her as she managed to stand, her face twisted by inner fury. Waves of intense hatred from Sue washed over me. I knew, if she managed to keep control of the gun, I was dead and then the others would be next. I had to take it from her. I had no choice.

It was as if the world was moving in slow motion. I took two steps backward as I raised the gun until it was level with her midsection. Without thinking, I pulled the trigger twice. Two loud bangs echoed off the walls and Sue's eyes went wide as she stumbled backward, gasping for breath. My nostrils and mouth were suddenly invaded by the smell of burnt gunpowder mingled with the iron scent of blood.

Sue clutched her stomach with both hands. Dark red blood seeped between her fingers. I froze. She looked at me, her eyes wide, the pain behind them making me want to wretch. I couldn't believe I'd shot my friend. God, what have I done?

I lowered the weapon, letting it fall from my grip. It rattled as it struck the floor. "Sue, I'm so sorry."

Sue's mouth hung open as blood started to trickle from the right side of her mouth.

She dropped to her knees, then collapsed onto her bottom with a cry of pain. She moaned softly. I knelt beside her and wrapped one arm around her shoulders as she dropped backward. I sat on the floor, cradling her head in my lap. She looked up at me, her watery eyes filled with pain. Her mouth moved but I couldn't make out most of the words except for "Sorry."

Her eyes closed and her head lolled to one side as the air escaped from her lungs for the last time. I hugged her to me and began to cry, salty tears rolling down my cheeks.

"I'm sorry, so sorry, Susie, I didn't...." I was about to say I didn't mean to kill her, but that wasn't true. I'd had to stop her even if it meant killing her. It was like shooting a rabid dog. Sue had gone off the mental cliff and she wouldn't have come back. She could have killed us all.

I eased her off my lap and let her limp body roll on its side in the pool of blood that had formed around her before her heart stopped. I wiped the tears away from my eyes and stood.

A rush of anger formed a knot in my belly. Those bastards were at fault. They forced us to turn on each other. A lot of good people, a lot of Sue's, would still be alive if they hadn't come to our planet. Goddamned aliens.

***

The cement floor of the warehouse made the interior of the vast empty building cooler than the humid air outside. I had my eyes closed as I fanned myself with one hand, grateful for the relief from the oppressive summer heat bearing down on the harbor beyond the open bay doors lining both sides of the structure. The warehouse sat at the end of a long pier, jutting out into the bay.

A cry of gulls filled my ears. I opened my eyes to gaze out the open bay door nearest me and spotted the gray wings of the snow-white birds circling above the overturned and burned-out ships floating untended in the oily water in the bay. Like the water, the air was still; but I could smell the rotting flesh of dead fish and human corpses entombed in those shattered vessels. The stench used to make me gag but I was well past that now—I was getting used to the odors of death. I'd seen too much of it in the past six weeks, more than most soldiers saw in a year on the battlefield. But we were on the frontline of the fight for survival, and one consequence was witnessing things no one should have to.

"Liz," called a man's voice from behind my left shoulder. I shifted on the steel chair to face him—Al Hamburg, in his battle armor, hefting his assault rifle. His curly blond hair stuck out from the edges of a Kevlar helmet and dark sunglasses covered his eyes. His torso, arms, and legs were protected by body armor. He nodded at me when I didn't reply and disappeared from view behind the warehouse wall where he would stand guard until he escorted me back to the neighborhood. We were five miles from the barricades but I knew Al and his team would protect me. They had accompanied me from the barricade, where they'd shown up to escort me to this meeting. Professional soldiers always follow orders, so I wasn't worried.

Al was the commander of an elite Special Forces unit recruited by the Hsu-Zat to act as bodyguards when they visited our planet's surface. The Hsu-Zat had arrived in Earth orbit six weeks ago and immediately used some form of advanced electromagnetic pulse weapon to take out our technology worldwide. The weapon even used our satellites to send the pulse that threw civilization back into the dark ages. I missed my damned cell phone more than I should. I must have been addicted to the thing.

Airliners dropped from the sky, creating massive destruction and loss of life. Military forces so dependent on technology found themselves and their weapons useless. Even the most EMP-hardened technology was ineffective in preventing this alien weapon from taking it out. The world had gone all to hell, and all that stood between anarchy and order was the neighborhood watch.

I know all this because, for some reason, a Hsu-Zat who called himself Robert—he told me his real name would be unpronounceable—decided I would be the spokesperson for my neighborhood. We'd met regularly, once per week, for the past six weeks. I'd never asked why he chose me, and frankly I didn't care.

The odd thing was Robert answered any question I asked him and had since our first meeting. As far as I could tell, everything he told me was accurate. The human tendency to lie to protect personal feelings didn't seem to apply to these aliens. He casually related the death toll numbers caused by their suppression of our technology and by the disruptions in civil order that soon followed.

If he considered my circumstances dire in any way, he hadn't let on. In fact, Robert had been cold but not unkind to me.

That's why I'd left my knife behind, the one I had intended to use to slit his throat as retribution for Sue's death. Even if I managed to kill him, one alien's death wouldn't mean much in the scheme of things.

From one of the open bay doors, Robert entered, flanked by two others of his kind. His crimson-colored features were placid, his two mustard-yellow eyes avoiding me as his brown boots slapped the concrete floor. The sound of the three aliens' footsteps echoed off the high walls. Other than their skin color, they were humanoid: two arms, two legs, everything in the same places as us. It had been difficult for me to distinguish one alien from another until I noticed the small scar on the end of Robert's pointed chin. He later told me this was due to a childhood fall without elaborating further.

His dark blue slacks and brown vest covered a frame that looked lean and strong, yet his voice had always been gentle, reminding me of the sound of a stream rushing over a rocky bottom. His arms were bare, as was his hairless head. His ears were relatively human shaped, the curvature at the top slightly elongated. His companions were dressed in identical garb. There must have been a big sale on alien fashions at the Hsu-Zat Walmart.

Robert stopped in front of me. His long arms, hanging loosely at his sides, ended with elongated fingers near his knees. Neither he nor his escorts had even been seen carrying weapons. Ray guns obviously aren't his team's thing.

One of his escorts went to grab another steel chair from ten feet across the warehouse floor. He carried it back, placing it behind Robert, who immediately sat, his eyes finally landing on mine.

"Hello, Elizabeth," he said in his usual monotone.

"Robert," I said with a slight nod of my head.

His eyes crinkled slightly at the corners. "I am saddened to learn of Susan's death."

I don't know how he knew, but Al probably told him before the meeting. I had learned not to trust those Special Forces guys. As far as I was concerned, they were the aliens' pets.

His words seemed genuine. Robert had either won the Hsu-Zat equivalent of the best actor Oscar or he meant what he'd said. I prefer to think it was the latter because he had never before shown any remorse for the deaths they had caused. At our next meeting, I decided, I would reverse my earlier decision. This son of a bitch was dead. I would probably die too, but the satisfaction would be better than a gold card with an unlimited credit limit.

"I am leaving," Robert said next.

"But you just got here," I said sarcastically.

Robert hesitated and his eyes shifted to an open bay door to his right and the ocean beyond. I glanced out the door. The wind had picked up and small swells had formed in the harbor. The cooling breeze brushed my right cheek. I detected the now familiar smells of almonds and orange coming from the aliens as the wind swirled through the warm air of the warehouse.

Robert's yellow eyes finally drifted back to mine. "Please forgive me. I meant we are leaving for home earlier than expected."

May's words echoed in my mind and my heart skipped a beat. "You said we had ninety days then you'd turn the power back on."

Robert nodded. "Yes, I did, but my orders have changed. I must return home immediately." The alien stared at me, his eyes pleading. He was unable to elaborate. I glanced at his companions and saw them standing stiff as soldiers at attention, their eyes focused straight ahead looking into the distance, appearing uninterested in our conversation. But I knew they were very interested and listening to every word.

"Will you at least turn the power back on?"

Robert shook his head. "No, that is beyond our capability."

I pursed my lips as my gut tightened. The bastards told us when they destroyed the grids they would restore them after ninety days. It hadn't made sense at the time, but what choice did we have but to believe them. Obviously they lied. "When are you leaving?"

"Immediately," he said again. He paused and I could tell his next words were very uncomfortable for him. I braced myself for the worst. "There are nuclear power generating facilities all across your world that are going critical without the power grid. These facilities will soon melt down and send clouds of radioactive material into your atmosphere. Unfortunately, this means all life on your planet will be extinguished."

My stomach churned and my emotions threatened to overwhelm me. Fear, anger, love, hate ebbed and flowed through my mind. "Then what was the ninety days all about?"

For the first time since I'd met him, Robert appeared flustered. His features were a darker red, his skin now the color of pomegranate juice. His hands trembled and his eyes sagged, reflecting a very human sadness. "I'm sorry," he said again. "Orders."

Neighborhood Watch

I nodded and sighed. He wasn't a bad guy for an alien. "Okay, Robert." I stood and his two companions suddenly stepped between us. I smirked at the three aliens, then turned and walked away.

The ninety days was in realty a countdown. A countdown to doomsday. The Hsu-Zat had known all along what would happen after they shut down everything. Their arrival was an experiment and we were the guinea pigs.

Once the human race was extinct, the aliens would eventually have a green and fertile planet to colonize without interference from the indigenous population. Sure, it would take time for the Earth's ecosystems to regenerate, but the Hsu Zat had all time in the universe. Our time had run out. Maybe Sue was one of the lucky ones.

I was determined to delay our impending doom, at least in my little corner of the world. The neighborhood watch would continue maintaining some semblance of civilization until the end came. We weren't going quietly into the night.

While it was more likely we'd destroy ourselves before the radioactive clouds killed us, the neighborhood watch would forestall the inevitable as long as possible. Our neighborhood would stand alone if need be.

As for me, I was determined to be the leader I was born to be. I wasn't about to give the Hsu Zat our neighborhood without showing them we still had fight left in us. It's what we humans do.

When I was a kid becoming a superhero seemed like a really, really cool idea. These teens experience this for real and soon discover the responsibility that comes with their newly acquired powers.

Clubhouse Heroes

The air in Spike Arnold's father's garage reeked of sweat and was hotter than the middle class neighborhood of bungalows and split level houses surrounding his parents three bedroom bungalow on Spence Street. My parent's house was two blocks over on Chamberlain Lane. No doubt it wouldn't be any cooler, or warmer for that matter, than Spike's place. But we couldn't meet at my house. My older sister and brother were jerks who treated my friends like they were super annoying cold sores. At least they had the super part right.

Though Mr. Arnold had converted the garage to a workshop the enclosed room still had a slight smell of gasoline and oil.

No doubt the cement floor had absorbed the oil and gas leaks from the cars parked in here since the house was built in the 1950's. At least that's what Spike claimed when one of the guys brought it up at a previous meeting.

But we all knew Mr. Arnold was a lazy butt. He hadn't bothered to fix up the workshop properly. Instead he built it fast and as cheap as possible with a wobbly wooden workbench against one wall constructed from two by fours and a sheet of three quarter inch plywood he ripped off from a construction site. There were six wooden kitchen chairs that creaked when we sat on them he found at the dump. He never built anything in here at least as far as we knew so we used it as our clubhouse.

The truth was the workshop was Mr. Arnold's hide out from Spike's mother who had the reputation as the neighborhood witch. Mrs. Arnold was always angry frequently yelling at us kids for riding our bikes too fast, or screaming at us when we laughed too loud as we walked past her house on the way home from school. Yeah, she's a real piece of work.

The garage had its secrets not the least of which was Mr. Arnold's stack of Playboys we boys found in a dusty, rotting cardboard box in one corner, and his stash of empty whiskey bottles behind the water heater in another box with not a drop of booze in them. Believe me we checked each bottle and they were dry. No wonder he didn't get any work done in the garage with all this wonderful soft porn and booze. The guy was only human after all.

Recently we admitted a girl into the club so Playboy's had given way to hair the color of copper, pale cheeks dotted with freckles, and a laugh that made you smile even if you were having a shit day. Too bad she didn't laugh much.

Her name is Izzy—short for Isabelle—Creek. For the first time in my life I fell in love at first sight with this vision of girlhood. This skinny, gangly girl may have a chip on her shoulder the size of the empire state building, but I had fallen hard for her. Every time I saw her at school or at one these weekly meetings my mouth dried and my heart beat faster every time I saw her.

Naturally she had no idea about my feelings, nor had I shared my need to kiss Izzy with the guys. The teasing would have been constant and merciless.

In preparation for today's meeting I grabbed a chair from where they were lined up in front of the wall of rakes and shovels and garden hoes standing in the makeshift rack comprised of nails banged into a two by four which was screwed into the wall. The handle of tool was placed between two nails nailed close together so it wouldn't fall over. I set the chair in the center of the cement floor avoiding a large oil stain on the gray cement.

Us guys are thirteen now having grown up in the neighborhood together, played sports together, fought bully's together, went to the movies together, ya know all the guy crap. But now that Izzy had entered our world I sensed things were about to change. Especially since we all had super powers now.

Our health class teacher, Mrs. Isometric, told us puberty would be a bitch (well maybe not those exact words), but she never prepared us for spontaneously developing superpowers after our thirteenth birthdays. Catholic boys and girls have the Sacrament of Confirmation when they come of age. Jewish boys become a bar mitzvah usually at thirteen while Jewish girls become a bat mitzvah at twelve. What the hell do you call a super hero when they mature and gain their powers?

Super charged?

I hadn't told anyone about my powers because I am the largest boy physically in the club at five feet six inches tall with a wide chest and muscular arms and legs sprouting hair already. I'm still a little clumsy. My parents say I had a summer growth spurt which is why I'm so much bigger than the other kids my age, but Im so embarrassed after gym class when we have to use the communal showers.

The real problem though is my *gifts* don't fit my appearance.

I'm able to extend small sticky hairs from the palms of my hands and the soles of my feet using them to climb walls as easily as an insect. I would say the words human fly to describe my talents but it's sooo embarrassing that the biggest guy in the club represents the smallest creature on the planet.

Now me being able to climb walls without ropes or any gear may seem cool, and truthfully by itself it wouldn't be so bad, but there's more. I'm project empathy onto others.

The first time it happened I projected empathy onto my big sister, Maxine—known by her more common moniker, Max—when our cat died.

My sister, fifteen going on thirty-five, is a stoned cold bitch with a bad attitude who can burn toast with her eyes. Literally.

I fully expected one day the club would have to fight her since I knew my creep of a sister is going to be a super villain and try to take over the world.

Anyway, as dad carried poor dead Scraps to the car to take him to the vet for disposal Max was being a real rat bag referring to Scraps as a fleabag whose best friends were the filthy mice inhabiting the falling down garden shed in our back yard.

Now this may be true, Scraps had been a lazy cat, but I was still pissed at her so I projected empathy onto her. While her attitude changed immediately, and she went with dad to the vet to drop off the kitty corpse, she returned home with fire in her eyes intending to sizzle my ass like an over done steak.

Somehow she knew what I had done to her.

To escape her death rays I climbed the tallest cedar tree in the heavily wooded green space down the street from our house. She needed time to cool off. Breathing hard the smell of tree sap filling my mouth and nose I knew all I had done was delay our eventual showdown, but like in the movies older sisters eventually forgive their younger siblings, or so I hoped.

Spike and I were the only ones to arrive so far for today's meeting. Spike's blond hair was styled in what's known as Liberty Spikes. The name is meant to be synonymous with the Statue of Liberty. The spikes run down from the front center of the head in a straight line to the nape of the neck, the hair on the sides is shaved or cropped so short that the scalp is easily visible. The result looks like a crown similar to the one atop the Statue of Liberty. He'd colored the spiky hair purple. Spike is so awesome.

To complete his super hero persona Spike usually wore a black leather jacket, blue jeans, and leather boots the color of the charcoal briquettes my father burned at in his barbecue grill completing his scary look.

Today was hot so he'd doffed his leathers in favor of a white tee shirt, black shorts, and open toed back plastic sandals on his narrow feet.

Spike's talent is the ability to fly so he can swoop down on people as if he were a giant crow with spikes on his head. He'd even developed a screeching cry to augment his fierce look. Anyone who heard his shrill cry for the first time usually wet themselves, which he really liked and made me laugh.

So far his guise as Liberty Spike had worked perfectly. He ran off a few baddies trying to steal old ladies purses outside senior's homes across the city.

Spike had become quite the celeb among the seniors set and they had a hell of a gettin'-the-word-out network amongst the retirement homes around the city to spread the word about his exploits.

In contrast the cops discouraged us saying The Clubhouse Heroes (as the news websites had taken to calling us) were vigilantes who took the law into their own hands. The city should have given the guys medals but the stupid jerks just didn't appreciate our talents and the cops resented them.

The dangerous side of the job stopped Spike and the others for going full on super. None of them were gifted with invulnerability.

Spike caught my eye and grinned before he snagged a chair for himself carried it to the center of the garage setting it next to mine. I could smell the spearmint gum on his breath as he walked past me. "You're early, comic book," he said as he plunked himself down on the chair causing it to creak in the still, warm air.

My real name is Bobby Strang but the guys call me comic book because I collect super hero comics.

I am the club consultant since I had an extensive collection of super hero comics going back to when I was five years old and my dad bought me my first one at a drug store. I'd been collecting comic books ever since.

The thought crossed my mind to call Spike Captain Obvious, but the side door leading to the walkway to the front door of the house burst open interrupting me before I could speak. The sound of familiar laughter wafted through the open door.

Ach, Izzy, and Mark had arrived. Besides it made no sense to piss off Spike as the keeper of the keys to our clubhouse.

When someone in the club discovered my collecting hobby on my Front Book page they asked me to join. I jumped at the chance to work with actual super heroes, it's a fantasy come true for me. None of the guys ever told me who spotted my page but I knew it had to be Mark. He reads minds, which is really cool in my opinion, but he says it's not all that great to read minds especially at school. Eighth grade politics can tear you up, man.

Mark Fasberg is black with thick short curls covering his nearly perfect round head. He wears wire-rimmed glasses and is of medium build.

Not overly muscular he plays left wing midfielder on the school soccer team so he's in pretty good shape.

Then there's Achmed Mahod (we call him Ach for short) whose family emigratted from Syria to the U.S. in the '70's. His special gift is his ability shoot water from his fingers that he can direct at any object or person he chooses. I don't know how he does this without drying up like the riverbed out near the old gravel pit, but he's great to have around on a camping trip when you need to extinguish the campfire. It saves your arms and hands from having to lug water in buckets for a stream or lake.

Of course the question we get asked all the time is do the guys, and Izzy, plan to use their gifts for good or evil. Since they don't know how to respond to this question they tell reporters and neighbors and our parents they have no idea explaining they're just kids. While the adults seem to accept this lame answer to what I think is very serious question I'm certain they're afraid they might end up on the dark side of the coin.

Knowing comic books like I do I'm not so sure myself.

These guys, and Izzy, have strong personalities and insecurities abound given we are pre-teens and uncertain where our lives are headed at the moment.

Speaking for myself I'm determined to be a good guy, not a villain.

"Hey, comic book," says Mark grabbing another chair from the ones left near the wall of tools. He grinned at me.

I nodded. "Hey, Mark, Ach, Izzy...good to see you guys..." My cheeks suddenly felt warm as I realized I had called Izzy a guy. She however didn't seem to notice my mistake her eyes cast downward as she grabbed a vacant chair and dragged it noisily across the cement floor until it was next one of the others we were setting up in a semicircle.

"Hey, Izzy," protested Spike, "my dad's gonna freak if you break that." He nodded at the chair. She smirked at him her eyes narrowing to slits and sat down with her arms crossed over her chest. She wore jean shorts and a bulky gray sweatshirt with a hood. On her feet were pink flip-flops.

"Let's get on with this. I got stuff to do," she said, her tone registering her annoyance.

Everyone including me sat down. I studied the features of the members of our little band of would be heroes each in turn. None of them looked particularly pleased to be here as if they had better things to do. Not that I blamed them they probably did. Most kids are over scheduled by their parents in some mistaken belief this will build character and lead to success in life. Like me these kids were ignored by their parents and were social outcasts in the pressure cooker known as high school.

In contrast to the others Mark was smiling and looked pleased with himself about something he'd no doubt learned when he read a mind. I wasn't going to be the first one to ask in case he had read mine and learned of my infatuation with the female in our midst. Mind readers are incredibly nosy about other peoples business.

Since the clubhouse was in Spike's garage he acted as chair for the meetings. Pulling out his cell phone to glance at the screen he nodded and emitted a soft grunt. "Okay, guys, it's 10 a.m. Saturday morning, July 3rd. tomorrow is the 4th of July."

Again with the Captain Obvious stuff. What was up with him? Was he trying to annoy us on purpose?

Izzy and Ach seemed fixated on the oil stain on the garage floor their expression blank and their eyes reflecting their lack of interest.

Spike's brow wrinkled and he glared at Mark. "What's so funny, bud?"

Mark chuckled generating stares from Ach and Izzy. At least they had finally joined the rest of us. "We finally have something we can do," said Mark.

I swallowed hard. Did he know about my secret ability?

"What?" said Spike clearly annoyed.

"There is going to be an attack at the picnic tomorrow in Grammer Park. We will stop it and catch the criminals who want to disrupt the picnic."

Izzy grunted. "What a load of shit, Mark. How do you know there's going to be an attack? And who are the criminals?"

Mark leaned back in the chair stretching his long legs out crossing his ankles and his arms. "I often walk or ride my bike around the neighborhood reading a few minds randomly. Yesterday I read the minds of the plotters. A girl and a guy."

"Where?" I blurted without thinking. This could be my chance to reveal myself to the club to make a real contribution.

Braised I really was interested. Ever since I'd learned of Mark's gift I'd wanted to be able to read minds. It must be awesome to hear other's people's thoughts in your head.

I froze when I realized all eyes were on me. I shrugged and offered a weak chuckle. "I mean what house or was it on the street? It'll help us find them."

Spike's mouth formed a sneer. "Comic book," he began with that voice my dad reserved for those times when I screwed up. My stomach tightened and anger rose in my throat. I really hate that voice.

"You won't be coming on the mission with us. We're the super powered heroes, all you do is provide stuff about what super heroes can do and not do." His eyes shot to Izzy then back to me. His lean frame relaxed. "Besides you might get hurt and we can't let that happen." He shrugged. "You're a member of the club," Spike added as if this explained everything.

They were blowing me off. They didn't respect me or the intelligence gathering I'd contributed to the club so far.

Spike directed his attention to Mark whose smile had faded. "Who are these criminals?"

Mark shrugged. "I'm not exactly sure because they're using super villain names. The girl is called Burnout and the guy is Projectile.

She can burn stuff with her eyes; he shoots
steel darts from devices strapped to the underside
of his wrists. According to my reads (mark calls
his mind reading *reads*) he made the devices after
stealing the designs for the technology from a DOD
computer system he hacked."

Izzy's eyes widened. "Military hardware?"

Matt nodded matter of factly. "Yeah.
Experimental stuff."

"What are they planning?"

Matt's brow wrinkled and his eyes narrowed.
"I'm not sure exactly only that it has something to do
with the 4th of July party at the park."

Spike rose to his feet and walked to a
blue plastic bin overflowing with newspapers and
advertising flyers. I thought about helping him but
remained seated when the others didn't offer. I'm a bit
of a follower that way. I volunteered once for hallway
monitor in elementary school and got beat up after
school almost every day until I quit. Following the
group was better than being the punching bag of the
week.

While Spike shuffled through the stack of old
newspapers Izzy stood up and went to the old fridge
in one corner of the garage where Spike's mom kept a
supply of soda in various flavors.

"Wan' one?" she said glancing over her shoulder at us before she opened the fridge door.

"Grape," said Mark. I asked for an orange. Ach wanted a diet cola. She brought back three cans including her fav, lemon lime. She tossed us our sodas then sat once again on the chair next to Ach. I secretly would have preferred her next to me, but this wasn't the right time. Some days I wondered if the right time would ever come.

"Aha," said Spike holding a newspaper triumphantly in his right hand.

Staring at Spike I pulled the aluminum tab to open the can of cold soda and took a long drink then said, (after first letting an orange flavored burp pass my lips) "Okay, what's the deal?"

Spike brought the newspaper over and dropped it on the seat of his empty chair. "Look at the headline." I leaned forward as did Izzy and Ach. I shared a look of horror with them after we scanned the large block lettering across the front page of the town paper. It read, MAYOR INVITES VICE PRESIDENT TO ATTEND JULY 4TH PICNIC.

Oh. My. American Idol.

**

After begging and pleading—I texted Mark, Spike, and Ach every ten minutes for the rest of the day until they agreed I should some—I convinced the guys to let me join the club at the park. Not that they could stop me, since this is a public event and I'm still part of the public.

What disappointed me the most was Izzy's attitude. She didn't seem to care if I came along or not. It was actually Mark who seemed to be the only one concerned about my safety.

Anyway, when we arrived at the park the place was jammed with people, their kids and dogs running wild all over the tramped down grass which probably would be dead until next spring. Not that this was my problem, but I enjoy green grass and the smell when it's fresh cut. All right I'm weird, what can I say?

There were families sitting on blankets or law chairs covering the park with an elevated platform containing a band consisting of three guys with guitars, a guy beating on some drums, and a girl who was the lead singer. When we arrived the band had just started playing old Beatle tunes. (My mom irons our clothes with the radio tuned to the oldies station.).

Under the branches of a stand of firs and oak trees beyond the picnickers was a row of gas barbecues cooking burgers, hot dogs, ribs, and polish sausages. My stomach grumbled when the smell of the grease and charred meat wafted over us. I only had a bowl of Toasty Oaties before heading for the park this morning so I was hungry.

"Strangely inappropriate that they're playing songs by a British rock group on the day we celebrate our independence from the Brits don't ya think?" murmured Izzy. I choked back a laugh and she glanced at me with a brief smile on her lips.

Surveying the chaos on this sunny day the sun beating down on us from a cloudless azure sky I didn't see anyone that could be described as a super villain. But they might not be dressed like the villains in the comic books. If they were smart they'd be dressed as if they were picnickers enjoying the day.

A guy dressed as a clown with a red nose, white face and blue hair wearing a baggy blue and green stripped one piece suit walked past me accompanied by someone dressed as Uncle Sam with a wig of white hair and a goatee wearing a red and white striped top hat with white stars on a blue band, a blue tail coat, and red and white striped pants.

Looking at their feet as they walked away from me I noticed something strange about them. They were wearing boots; work boots like construction crews wear on job sites. The day was hot and humid so wearing costumes would be uncomfortable enough so what gives with the work boots?

I moved to stand beside Mark who was focused on the barbecues in the distance a trickle of drool seeping from one side of his mouth. He was hungry too. You know what they say, breakfast of champions...or some such crap.

"Hey, Mark, do a read of those two." I indicated the clown and the Uncle Sam who appeared to be headed in the direction of the stage where no doubt the Veep and the mayor would be making their speeches. I really hate speeches because they're dull as the polish on my Sunday-go-ta-meetin' shoes, but I don't think anyone needs to be killed for making them, no doubt some people would disagree.

Mark looked at them and went silent. His eyes narrowed slightly. This was the only outward sign he was conducting a read of others people's minds which made him the perfect spy. If he weren't a decent guy I would have been worried he'd use his gift for bad stuff.

Izzy appeared on edge she was shuffling her feet while Ach was pretending to watch the baseball game going on at the ball field to out left. Spike had already taken off and was flying across the line of trees trying to avoid anyone seeing him. He was keeping under the shade of the branches and was dressed all in black so unless someone knew where to look they probably wouldn't see him. That was until we had to take action.

All around us were happy kids and teenagers their voices buzzing with shouts and laughter. Everyone was having fun except us.

My gut was tight with tension and I fixed my eyes on the retreating clown and Sam. Finally Mark spoke. "They're the ones alright." His tone was grim which is unusual for a happy go lucky guy like him. Mark shifted his gaze to me. "What are we gonna do?"

I had no idea realizing we hadn't taken the time to plan anything. I cringed inside. What lame ass heroes we turned out to be. How did we not think to plan something when we found the villains? Of course I don't think we ever truly believed we'd find them.

Not that we doubted Mark's abilities but until now he'd been good at finding lost keys and reading the answers for tests at school in the minds of the smart kids, ya know the ones who studied every night. Uncovering an evil plot to kill the vice president of the United States seemed a little far fetched even to me the comic book guy.

I shook my head. "I'm not sure," I said, my words sounded weak even to me.

"Well, we have to do something," chimed in Izzy.

Shifting to look at her I saw her lean body had tensed and her hand had formed fists at her sides. She still wore jean shorts with a fresh sleeveless forest green top, and she had doffed her preferred flip-flops the color of bubble gum in favor of black and gray tennis shoes. Running around a park battling super villains wearing flips flops didn't seem dignified or practical.

I knew she was right of course. I decided then I would take the direct approach. I set off after the clown and Sam moving quickly through the crowd of happy picnickers. Men holding beer cans, ladies in tube tops sunning themselves laying in blankets on the grass, children tossing balls, or playing tag their faces sticky with blue or pink cotton candy.

I dodged them all until I finally caught up with the villains who were nearing the band platform where the speeches were scheduled.

"Hey!" I shouted at the clown who didn't turn at the sound of my voice. Suddenly a large muscular body slammed into my side knocking the wind out of me and causing me to fall onto the grass.

Stars danced across my vision and I gasped for breath my side aching from the impact. A heavy weight pressed down on me pinning me to the ground.

"Hey!" I heard Izzy shout. "What the hell are you doing to my friend?"

The weight eased off me then disappeared as I managed to sit up coughing and sucking in air. My vision cleared and I saw a large man in a dark blue business suit standing over me his dark eyes glaring at me. "Secret service, ma'am," he said pulling a small black wallet from his inside suit pocket. He flashed a badge at identification card at me then put it back in his pocket.

"Why did you tackle him?" said Izzy her tone angry.

The man's already beady eyes narrowed. "I'm with the Vice President's protection detail and your *friend* was about to attack—" He stopped talking and his tanned cheeks flushed crimson.

"Move along." He started to walk away when he stopped and glanced back at us. "And don't come back." He hurried away and soon disappeared into the crowd.

I looked at Mark. "Is he for real?" I croaked in a harsh whisper.

Mark shrugged his expression sheepish. "Yeah, he's who he says he is. He was protecting the Uncle Sam. As I read it they caught Projectile and have an undercover agent infiltrating by wearing the get up he planned to use to get close to the Veep."

"So the Sam isn't a villain?" asked Izzy her eyes wide. Mark nodded. Izzy grunted. "How about the clown?"

He nodded. "Oh, yeah she's a super villain alright. She's comic books sister."

My heart skipped a beat. Max a super villain? Sure she's a real bitch on wheels but a super villain? "No way," I said. You must be wrong."

Mark pointed an index finger at the side of his head. "I might be but this is never wrong." Ach rolled his eyes. I was beginning to doubt him.

Suddenly a large black shadow swooped over us from above. Spike had returned from his spying. He landed next to me as Mark held out a hand to help me stand. My breathing had returned to normal.

"Why don't we just tell the secret service guy about the clown and let them take care of it."

"And let her kill them too?" I said. I'd seen my sister in action. She would burn them to ash before they could stop her.

"Why's the Veep coming to the picnic if there's an chance a super villain will try to kill him?" asked Izzy. It was a good question that none of us had the answer to. I could have asked the secret service guy if I could find him and he wouldn't kick my butt.

I knew then what we had to do.

An hour later with the arrival of the Veep's motorcade we had donned our disguises. We were disguised as clowns and stood behind the rope barriers set up to make a path fro the vice president and mayor to make their way to the stage. The secret service comprised of men and women in dark suits sunglasses covering their eyes flanked the stretch limo.

One agent opened the rear door and the Veep got out while the portly mayor exited the car on the other side. Man, is he fat.

The crowd of picnickers had lined up on both sides of the ropes to watch. They cheered as the Veep waved and smiled at the crowd.

She was prettier in person than on TV. Her blonde curls brushed the shoulders of her tanned suit jacket.

The mayor joined her standing to her left smiling with obvious pride as she greeted the crowd with obvious enthusiasm. Clearly she wasn't afraid of any super villains that might be lurking around.

Suddenly the clown we'd seen earlier burst through the crowd knocking over people like bowling pins until she leapt over a small boy to land on the makeshift pathway as if she were a cat facing the startled vice president. A female secret service agent stepped in front of the vice president as flames shot from the clowns eyes to engulf the agent in orange and red flames. She screamed as shouts of horror and fear erupted in the crowd.

Then, as if someone had fired a starter pistol at a big race, the picnickers scattered wildly running in all directions. Children screamed and shouts to look out holy mother of god help he's burning echoed chaotically over the park. A perfect 4th of July had suddenly become an orgy of panic, death and pain.

Ach shot water out of his fingers quickly dousing the flames on the secret service agent who had collapsed into a heap.

Simultaneously Spike had leapt into the air and landed hard on the deadly clown knocking her to the ground. He punched her in the face aiming in particular for the eyes hoping to stop her from setting him on fire too.

He kept punching until realizing he might kill her I moved to stop him grabbing his arm, as he was about to throw another punch. The makeup had fallen off her face and I saw my sister was unconscious, bruises already beginning to appear on her cheeks. Her eyes were swollen.

"Spike, take it easy. You don't want to kill her do ya?"

Spike looked at me his eyes blazing with fury. "Don't I?"

I patted his shoulder and he visible relaxed then climbed off my sister's prone form. We all wanted to avenge the brutal murder of the agent.

I glanced at the limo and saw the vice president inside her eyes wide before the tires screeched and the car drove away at high speed. I saw the mayor lying on his back next to the car with a first aid attendant pressing hard on his chest. I discovered later he'd had a heart attack. He was declared dead on arrival at the hospital.

Distant sirens began to fill the air getting louder with each passing second. I looked around at the clubhouse heroes, Izzy, Ach, Mark, and Spike. They were in shock but we had done our job. We stopped an assassination.

"Let's head for the clubhouse," I said softly.

They nodded in unison and we started to walk away trying not to be noticed. We dropped out clown disguises as we walked. No doubt the cops would be interested in anyone dressed as a clown for some time to come.

"What about your sister?" asked Izzy.

I looked back at my unconscious sister still lying on the trampled grass. I had no idea what would happen to her only that she would go to jail for a long time. I projected empathy toward her and hoped this time it would stick.

I stopped to gaze into Izzy's eyes. "I have something to tell you," I said.

Her eyes grew wider as I revealed my secret gifts to her and the others. They didn't tease me; in fact they welcomed me into the clubhouse heroes.

Sure our first mission had been successful but even success has a price.

One subgenre of horror that seems to be invincible in the public consciousness is the vampire tale. Perhaps it's the tantalizing possibility of immortality? This alternate history story demonstrates how immortality is not all its cracked up to be.

Unnatural Immortal

IN MID-AUGUST, NIGHTS IN THE TALL TIMBERS forest are muggy and stifling, the air thick as pudding. But the tranquility of this green meadow in the middle of these elegant pines and majestic oaks provided a welcome respite for Amy Selkirk, who sat almost buried in the long, wild grasses tipped yellow by the sun. Leaning back she rested her weight on her hands, relishing the peace and quiet of the dark woods surrounding her. But even the meadow's tranquility could do little to lessen the oppressive humidity of the summer and the danger that lurked around every tree.

She was bathing in this fleeting escape from the real world.

Amy lolled her head back with her eyes closed, dreaming of her revenge while the sweet odor of wildflowers filled her nostrils, the fragrant jasmine and lavender providing a pleasant distraction. In reality, she was unable to fully relish the peace this place of retreat promised for very long.

The unquenchable thirst gripping Amy's every waking hour was like a massive weight pressing on her by some unseen force. Too often these days the hunger for blood pushed away all other thoughts. Each passing day this need became more intense, threatening to consume her. Soon Amy's humanity would disappear, completely lost in a swirling vortex of lust and death that had become her new reality.

Time was growing short.

Her sire, Argos, the vampire who made her one of the undead, had preyed on her weaknesses and insecurity, using them as weapons to take control of her and her sister by offering her immortality. She agreed to become a vampire before she realized her romantic notions of immortality were false, the truth far more terrible than she imagined and far from romantic. Argos tricked her into this existence of living death.

Early on after her transformation, she struggled with her decision to challenge her sire until she came to realize Argos was a power-mad despot bent on building his own personal empire on the bloody, broken bodies of human cattle—the ultimate goal being his quest for absolute power. He had to be stopped before he enslaved the world to his will, and Amy was determined to destroy Argos before it was too late.

Sighing, she opened her eyes and turned her head slightly to look at the corpse, her prey, in the inky blackness of the night lying facedown buried in the grass next to her.

Amy had laid him next to her after carrying him across her shoulders up the hill to this meadow. His name was Edward Lamp; he had been a plantation owner from the nearby town of Andersonville.

The late Mr. Lamp bought his cotton from slave owners, men who exploited what she still thought of as her people. Slavery was an abomination that also had to end. Amy was determined to scour this inhuman practice from the face of the earth. Lamp would be the first of many who would die before her mission in this world ended.

Argos and her sister, Mary, must die if she was to save humanity from a terrible fate.

After arriving from Europe, Argos had made his fortune in the new world by growing cotton on the plantation he stole from its former owner after that owner disappeared under mysterious circumstances. Fellow plantation owners readily accepted Argos' explanation that the previous owner had fled to Europe after failing to make good on his debts. Argos generously paid for the man's passage back to his homeland and he assumed his plantation in exchange. Of course, these so-called *facts* were completely false. Amy knew Argos had killed the previous owner, burying the head and torso separately in his own cotton field.

Argos then had a copious supply of the fresh, iron-rich blood supplied by the many slaves on his plantation, but also from slaves of nearby farms. It also meant the number of vampires was growing exponentially all across the Confederate States of America, also known as the CSA, with Argos at the epicenter of death and terror.

Amy intended to control the supply of fresh victims from the source and restore the world to balance. At least as she saw balance.

In order for her plan to work, every existing vampire would have to be permanently dead.

As a one-woman army, she had the impossible task of tracking and killing all Argos' victims and their spawn. It reminded her of trying to stop ripples in a pond after dropping in a pebble. She needed help, which meant she needed a plan.

First she must build her own vampire army. Edward Lamp would be the tenth member of this army.

Her concern was it had been over one hundred fifty years since the Union failed to stop the Confederate States from over-running the country, so she had very real doubts about her own ability to stop Argos by herself when an entire nation had failed.

A more personal challenge she had to overcome was her remaining human aversion to taking human life. She abhorred killing the living.

Amy shivered at the memory of Argos sinking his fangs into her flesh, the wet sound of him puncturing her skin, his fangs tearing through the soft tissue of her neck, then the pain as they sank into an artery in order to drink her blood. She recalled the exhilarating mix of pain, ecstasy, and horror than ran through her as her lifeblood ebbed.

She also recalled the finality of the fading sight of the filthy room she shared with her sister Mary when the release of death finally enveloped her.

At the time, it seemed good to die.

The next thing she remembered was the warm, coppery taste of blood passing between her lips and the musty scent of iron in her nostrils. When she finished drinking her prey's thick life force, Amy sat back on her haunches on the straw mattress to discover, to her horror, she had killed her beloved sister.

Mary's stare at her with unseeing eyes still haunted her. Mary's motionless form, not breathing, a pale, waxy apparition, the side of whose neck was a ragged mess of torn skin, veins, and the oozing red wounds where Amy's fangs had ripped Mary's flesh was fresh in Amy's memory.

Gripped by the shock and horror of what she had done, Amy grabbed handfuls of her own hair and ripped them out, then threw back her head as a scream ripped from her lungs. Her body was wracked by deep, bone-shattering sobs as salty thick tears began to stream down her cheeks forming muddy rivulets on her cold, dead skin.

Yes, Amy would never forget Mary's ugly death until, in what seemed like only minutes but could have been hours or even days, her sister gasped and began to breath once again.

Amy watched Mary's breaths coming in short gasps as the wounds closed around tiny, round scabs of healing flesh. Mary's undead eyes slowly opened to reveal yellow eyes like those of a cat. Then her lips parted to reveal elongated incisors.

Mary licked her lips as her eyes narrowed and her once-dead gaze focused on Amy. "Hello, sister, should we feed?"

Amy realized immediately her beloved sister had become like Argos and herself. She had made Mary an undead monster spawned from hell. Her sister's death was on Amy's head. Now it was Amy's responsibility to end her beloved sister's immortality.

Unlike her sister, Amy had chosen to become a vampire. Her free will had resulted in a living death until the end of time.

Amy could have simply allowed the sun to dissolve her dead flesh, but so far she'd been unable to take her own life. What little humanity remained within her didn't want to die, not completely.

The irony was that once her humanity disappeared, the need to kill would be all she would lust after. All thoughts of her former life would be overwhelmed and she'd no longer be human. She'd witnessed these phenomena before.

Amy closed her eyes and shuddered at the image of the inhuman monsters she'd seen wandering the grounds of the plantation at night. Argos forbade his minions to attack his slave stock, but his neighbor's slaves were fair game.

Many slaves were reported missing but the humans assumed they had run off—a not uncommon occurrence with all the abusive plantation owners.

Posses of heavily armed men had been organized to locate the missing slaves, but so far none had been found.

Amy smirked to herself. She knew where Argos' prey slept during the day, but the humans would never believe her if she told them. After all, she was just another slave and vampires were a myth. The other still-human slaves thought she was a voodoo woman, so they avoided her as if she had the plague.

The buzz of an air patrol not far away and coming from the direction of the Hoover Mountains made her tense and sucks in a breath. Her eyes shot open and she shifted her gaze to look at Edward Lamp, still lying prone on the grass. Lamp hadn't been resurrected yet and there was no telling how long it would be before he arose.

This could be a problem.

Using her ability to see in the dark as if it were midday, Amy scanned the stands of trees ringing the perimeter of the meadow. She grunted when she found the perfect spot. A cave in the side of a hill would be the perfect place to store Lamp until he was resurrected. Amy would need him and she wasn't about to let the CSA Police have him, not when her plans were so close to nearing fruition.

Grabbing Lamp's body, she tossed him over her left shoulder and carried him to the cave. Just after they entered the cover of the cave, a beam of white light lit up the meadow as if it were midday rather than two in the morning, forcing Amy to cover her eyes with her arms. The real sun would rise in just over three hours so she hoped the air patrol would have moved on well before then.

"Amy Selkirk," said an amplified voice, "we know you're there. Reveal yourself."

Doubts invaded Amy's consciousness, causing her to hesitate. How had they found her? She had been careful to mask her movements and hiding places during the daylight hours. Maybe someone saw her take Edward Lamp?

If she failed to respond, no doubt the CSA Police would begin carpet-bombing the meadow.

The bombs would definitely kill her but would also destroy Edward's corpse and she needed him the world needed him alive a little longer. Until the rebellion ended Argos was the eye of this hurricane of terror. He would be the last to be destroyed then vampirism would end forever and the CSA would be finally defeated.

"Turn off the light and I'll come out," Amy said, shouting to be heard over the roar of the air car's twin turbines that held it aloft on a cushion of air.

The pilots must have heard her because the searchlight blinked out leaving only the craft's soft, indigo running lights to illuminate the meadow.

The air car then floated to the ground, landing on its tripod undercarriage, the engines' roar quickly diminishing, then stopping altogether as the craft came to rest on the grass.

The side cargo door swung upward on hydraulic arms accompanied by the soft whir of the motors. Immediately two armed CSA police troopers burst out onto the squashed grass, dressed in head to foot gray and green battle armor, the faceplates closed, their automags scanning the area around them ready to fire on anyone foolish enough to attack.

From bitter experience, Amy knew the troopers' weapons were loaded with rounds that would shred her into fleshy ribbons of bloody meat that even her ability to heal would be useless against. The CSA had learned the most efficient method to destroy a vampire without holy water or wooden stakes. Those ancient weapons against the undead were a thing of the past. Why risk close and personal? Why not kill from a safe distance?

Amy shuddered as she recalled several friends who had been shredded by CSA weapons, their flesh peeling off their bones, then burned to ash as she watched in horror. And Argos standing beside her, a sly grin on his lips as his police force murdered her friends. The choking stench of burnt flesh still filled her nostrils, accompanied by the wisps of charred remains carried by the wind, created by the swirling fires that seemed to invade every orifice of her body and cling to her clothing for days after.

Amy's eyes flitted to Lamp, who had yet to arise; then she stumbled out of the cave mouth, walking toward the two heavily armed police troopers with their weapons trained on her.

Her breath caught in her throat when she saw Argos, dressed in his usual head-to-toe black clothing.

His shoulder-length, slick, shiny black hair was pulled into a tight ponytail revealing his angular features. He stepped out of the air car with her sister by his side. Mary's yellow eyes glinted in the running lights of the air car.

"Mary?" Amy said after coming up short. Her heart beat hard and her hands trembled. The old fears and doubts re-surfaced from deep within her.

Amy had sworn revenge when she learned Argos had planned from the beginning to make her change her sister into one of the undead. And she vowed to free her sister from the curse she had inflicted on her. Argos detested love in all its forms, even between siblings. His intention all along had been to make an example of the two sisters to the rebellious slaves by having Amy curse her beloved sister, Mary, with vampirism, demonstrating anyone could be made to turn on anyone, even their own beloved ones.

A knot of pure hatred burned within Amy as Argos, with a knowing smile on his thin, bloodless lips, his manner cocky, approached. Her hands formed fists at her sides and she fought the urge to strike out at the bastard.

"Hello, my dear," he said in his deep voice as he and Mary drew near.

Amy wanted to tear him open and gut him like a melon but she held back when a furtive glance at the troopers confirmed they still had their weapons trained on her. They'd burn her down before she could finish one step toward their master. She knew they were also vampires so their reflexes would be as good as her own.

"Hello, Argos," she said, her eyes shifting to look at Mary's ash gray face, then back to lock eyes with Argos. She was determined not to show him any fear or surrender to his will. With herculean effort, Amy had thus far managed to retain a portion of her humanity, making it difficult for Argos to control her, and she vowed to never let him control her or anyone else again.

But she also knew eventually her free will would disappear with her humanity. She fought against his power as much as she was able, but being this close to him chipped away at her inner defenses like a pick at a block of ice.

Argos reached into the pocket of his knee-length black pea coat and withdrew an ivory pipe. Placing the tip between his lips, he extracted a shiny, gold-plated lighter from his other pocket and after lighting it used the yellow flame to light the tobacco in the bowl of the pipe.

He puffed and the contents glowed as smoke rose from the pipe. Amy could smell the rum-soaked tobacco.

After putting the lighter back in his coat pocket, he placed his free hand behind him and stared at her, puffing on his pipe, his inky gaze studying her. A sense of unease grew inside Amy with each passing second of silence.

Finally he spoke. "So we seem to have reached an impasse, my *dear* Amy. I gave you what you asked for and then you betrayed me. Is this the way for one of my children to garner my favor?"

Amy snorted. "You made me kill my sister...turn her into a monster..." Her voice disappeared behind a wall of rising anger.

Argos' brow furrowed and his eyes became hard. He tapped out his pipe into the grass, some of the embers still glowing, then placed it back in his coat pocket. She could sense his seething anger. "Amy, you're planning an insurrection against me. That is a violation of my trust and very disappointing."

Amy froze, startled by his words. She realized he should have killed her as soon as she appeared from the cave but he hadn't. Why?

"I should be dead...we all should be..."

"I think you know better than to say such a thing to me." Argos moved closer to her, giving the impression of him swooping down on her as if he were a bird of prey, which in a sense he was.

Amy took a step backward but in her mind she decided to stand firm. She glanced at her sister, who had an expression of wonder on her face that mingled with fear in her eyes. Then Amy looked back at her now furious former master.

It occurred to her that his anger made him weak; he had not realized he had stepped within her kill zone. She was about to throw caution to the wind and launch herself at Argos, intending to tear out his throat, when a man's voice from behind her caused her to hesitate.

'What's going on out here?" It was Edward Lamp, finally resurrected from death.

Argos stepped out of Amy's range as his features relaxed. "Nothing of consequence, my *dear* friend." His deep voice heavy with sarcasm. "You are just in time to see me deal with a traitor."

Amy turned her head to look at Lamp. "He means I'm a traitor for buying into his plans to change the entire world into his personal vampire army with him as absolute ruler."

Lamp, a big man over six feet tall, with broad shoulders and muscular arms, smirked. His thick body was now primed with the additional physical strength that came with becoming a vampire. He strode across the meadow, his wide face becoming more serious with each step. Finally he stood between the two armed troopers. He swept them both off their feet with his massive arms. They landed hard on their backs and lay still as their guns slipped from their grasps.

"I may have just changed the odds," he said, grinning at Amy.

Amy's eyes narrowed as she shifted her gaze to Argos, whose eyes were wide. This was something he hadn't expected.

Instead of fighting them, Argos turned and ran for the air car, which had already started its engines. It took off as soon as Argos had leapt aboard, the door closing behind him.

Coward, thought Amy.

"Thank you, Lamp," she said, turning to face her newly minted creation. "I'm sorry I turned you, but as you saw, it was necessary." Or at least she hoped he realized the severity of the situation.

At the end of the day, Lamp would have either been made a vampire by her or by Argos.

It seemed he appreciated her cause, especially seeing how Argos had reacted to his sudden appearance.

"So what is the deal between you and Argos?" Amy asked Lamp as she moved to wrap one arm around her sister's shoulders. Amy was pleased when Mary didn't flinch but instead pressed her body against her side.

Lamp emitted a deep-throated chuckle. "I've never liked the son of a bitch. More than once I threw him off my land when I caught him sniffing around my slave huts."

Amy's stomach tightened at his use of the word slave. She'd momentarily forgotten this man had been as despicable as any owner of enslaved human beings.

The grin slowly faded from Lamp's square-jawed features as his expression became serious and his eyes narrowed. "I knew what he was and I wasn't about to let him take any of my workers. I treated them well and protected them from the bloodsuckers as best I could." He shrugged slightly, then continued. "Argos swore to kill me but every time he appeared I managed to drive him off. I used fire, wooden stakes, crosses, garlic...everything at my disposal to stop him." His brow furrowed.

"Of course, now that I'm one of you, I don't know if I'll be able to continue protecting my people."

Amy's breath caught in her throat and her heart seemed to skip a beat. "What do you mean, your people?"

"I'm one quarter black on my grandmother's side. I inherited the plantation and vowed to treat the workers fairly and pay them. So far I've been able to keep my promise."

Amy's mind whirled with uncertainty and doubt. He could be lying. She had never heard of a plantation owner in the CSA paying slaves. Why had she not heard of this? "You're lying," she said, firmly convinced her words were true.

Lamp's wide face reflected his anger and his large, meaty hands formed fists. "No, I'm not." Amy watched as the anger in his eyes slowly faded, his features relaxed, and his fists unclenched. "I had to keep what I was doing secret or the other plantation owners would have told my buyers, who would have had me blacklisted. Not that I'm that concerned about money, but the loss for my workers would be far more than my personal fortunes would be able to afford." He sighed and turned his back to her as a breeze sprung up carrying with it the scent of the pine trees north of the meadow.

What Lamp was saying actually made sense. Amy made a decision knowing time was growing short. Argos wasn't about to let her get away again. He would end this once and for all—as far as he was concerned, at least.

"Lamp—"

Lamp turned back to face her with a grin on his lips, his gray eyes sparkling. "Call me Ed; everyone does."

Amy smiled to herself. She had taken a liking to this big man. "OK, Ed. I'm going to stay here with my sister. I urge you, beg you, actually, to continue the fight I started to destroy Argos."

Ed Lamp didn't say anything for several seconds, his eyes flitting between her and Mary. "What about you two?"

"Argos has no doubt ordered this area to be carpet bombed. In fact, I don't think you've got much time to make it to safety before a fleet of air cars arrives. Mary and I will stay behind and act as decoys so you can get away."

His words suggested he'd agree, but Amy needed to know for sure. "Ed. Will you do as I ask?"

Ed's eyes became hard and he nodded, his mouth a grim line of determination. Amy was satisfied.

As if to confirm his acceptance of her mission, he then stepped up to take her right hand in his. "I wish you well in the next world." His now sad eyes shifted to Mary, then back to her. "Both of you."

With those final words, Ed Lamp released her hand and ran toward the tree line, soon disappearing into the darkened tangled forest of trees beyond.

Amy watched until Ed was out of sight and she couldn't hear him in the brush any more, then turned to focus her attention on Mary. Moving to stand in front of her sister, Amy put her hands on Mary's shoulders.

"What are we going to do?" asked Mary, her eyes curious.

A single tear ran from Amy's left eye down her cheek. "My unnatural immortal, I'm about to release you from the curse." Amy swallowed hard. "But don't worry, we'll see each other again soon." The iron scent of Mary's tainted blood filled her nostrils as she bent closer to her sister's ivory skinned neck steeling herself to deliver the killing bite.

"Oh," was Mary Selkirk's last word as Amy sunk her fangs into her sister's neck and ended her undead existence.

Her sister's body sagged in her arms as air escaped Mary's lungs for the last time; the sound was quickly drowned out by the roar of multiple turbines that shattered the meadow's tranquility. The police fleet of air cars had arrived to bomb them into the next world.

Amy's heart was finally at peace as the bombs began to fall, secure in the knowledge Ed Lamp would exact revenge for not only her but for the countless people suffering from the curse placed on them by Argos and his undead horde.

Time travel, pirates, and secret agents? Hey, why not end this collection with a thrilling adventure on the high seas? Hope you enjoy the ride.

Bloody Betty, Queen of the Pirates

THE MOMENT ALOHA ENTERED THE CARIBBEAN Islands Holiday Theme Park, she wondered if today would be a bad day. Overgrown, tropical undergrowth bordered a small plot of land. Only a collapsed sign at one end of a pothole-filled gravel parking lot marked the wreck as anything other than more Nowhere, Florida.

Aloha pulled the strap of her handbag up onto her shoulder. *Gravel is hell on high heels. I should have switched to my sneakers.*

The amusement park was hardly the exciting, international destination the Legal Investigative Protection Service's recruitment brochure had promised. Knots of gnarled Cyprus trees guarded the theme park's perimeter.

Why did Simon have to send me here?

Hard to believe Director Mynass would send her to Sopchoppy, Florida after her last assignment in Paris. *France was soooo cool.*

This time the assignment e-mail read:

> WORK UNDERCOVER AS A CARNEY.
> IDENTIFY AND STOP A BIG UNDERWORLD
> TERROR AND TYRANNY SOCIETY AGENT
> FROM DESTROYING THE WORLD.

Another save the world job? Simon had given her so many of these assignments she sometimes thought it was all she would ever do. *Why always me?*

Sometimes it was a curse, being so good at her job.

France had been amazing. *But Sopchoppy? Maybe he hates me or something.*

Of course, she was just being silly. Simon respected his agents, her included.

But still, she missed the City of Light, the Eiffel Tower, the Seine, and the outdoor cafes where tourists could sip fragrant tea while nibbling on delicate, buttery pastry.

A mosquito the size of a Buick buzzed near her face. She swatted the vampiric insect away. *Another reason I hate this place—bloodsuckers.* She rolled her eyes. Why did her assignments so often have to include bugs or snakes or giant monsters?

Six attractions dotted the small theme park property—a Ferris wheel, a roller coaster, a Tilt-A-Whirl, a merry-go-round, a house of mirrors, and a large cave-like building.

The visible metal surfaces of every ride were coated in crimson rust. To her right, maybe fifty feet away, beside the Ferris wheel, squatted what Aloha supposed was the haunted house; at least it appeared to be a haunted house. As far as she was concerned, a few cobwebs over moss-covered, gray, weathered boards didn't exactly qualify as a haunted house, but it was as close as it got out here in the Florida sticks.

A building with a sagging sign identifying it as the house of mirrors also stood on the right side of the park. A cracked mirror was propped next to the entrance.

Her study of the park finally ended at the cave-like Bloody Betty, Queen of the Pirates ride next to the house of mirrors. Her cover was to be Bloody Betty, the pirate the ride was named after. The smooth, baby-blue painted, wooden trough coming out of the dark tunnel of the building suggested the ride had once had a river running from it. But that had been in the past.

Aloha's brow wrinkled. She didn't want to go near the thing. It didn't look safe.

The things I sometimes do for my job.

A soft breeze brushed over her cheeks. Her nose wrinkled under the assault of the combined stench of rotting wood and mud.

Yuck. This joint smells like wet dog butt.

The theme park was in such a sad state that it wasn't a wonder she didn't see any patrons. The real question was who would build a theme park in a remote place like this? And why would L.I.P.S. intelligence think the B.U.T.T.S. would send one of their operatives to this backwater? Like the B.U.T.T.S. would waste an X-Factor bomb on a run-down theme park?

I hardly think so, she mused. A dump like this wasn't a high-value target for terror. She crossed her arms and frowned. It was days like this when it seemed she was a dog chasing its tail. *I'm headed to nowhere land.*

Simon had never sent her anywhere without a good reason, so this particular dump had to be hiding something beneath its rusting exterior. But what?

"Can I help, ya?" said a gruff voice coming from her right.

Aloha dropped her arms to her sides and tensed. She spun toward the voice but didn't see anyone. "Hello?" Her tone had an edge of uncertainty. Her heart beat hard in her chest. Where was he?

"Up here." The voice now came from above her.

The mossy tendrils in the tree next to her began to wave about frantically. The branches drooped to the ground.

Her innate curiosity made her take a step back and peer hard into the tree branches.

On a thick, knotted gray branch sat a very small man, his legs crossed at the ankles. He grinned at her. He had brilliant, sea-green eyes, flame-red hair, and a matching full red beard. He certainly wasn't moss. He looked like a leprechaun. Or what she imagined a leprechaun would look like. His impish grin reminded her of the leprechaun character on the box of marshmallow-laced breakfast cereal she'd loved as a girl. He wore blue denim coveralls, which didn't exactly fit the image of a mythical Irish elf, so she surmised he was just a short guy with red hair.

"Huh, hello, are you Mr. O'Lanigan? My name's Aloha Armstrong."

The man's face was a mass of orange freckles and bore a wide smile. He stood with a speed that surprised her, then leapt into the air, seemingly floating above the branch, and did a perfect end-over-end flip. He landed on his feet in front of her, his arms extended from his sides. He stood at least three feet shorter than her. But at five-foot-nine, she was tall for a woman.

"Hello, Miss Armstrong. Yes indeed, I'm O'Lanigan, but you can call me Stinky. Everyone does." He smiled and waved his arms in the direction of the theme park. With a theatrical flourish, like one of those television models on game shows.

His eyebrows wiggled comically. "Nice theme park, don't ya think?"

Aloha grinned sheepishly. She didn't want to insult him on her first day undercover. Her work as an international secret agent was hard enough without the addition of annoying the locals. "Uh, yeah, I guess so?"

Stinky laughed. "No, it's not; it's crap." He held up one index finger. "But one day, mark my words, this theme park will be the center of the new Florida. One day I'll be bigger than Walt Disney."

"Yeah, right," she said sarcastically, without thinking.

Stinky's face turned crimson, and he scowled at her.

Time to change the subject. "Anyway, I'm here about the job?"

Stinky's cherub cheeks puffed out, and his mouth formed a wide smile again. "Good. Good. You're going to be Bloody Betty, Queen of the Pirates. Follow me."

He turned to walk away, heading in the direction of the Bloody Betty ride. Aloha hurried after him. Though he was small, he walked very fast.

The Bloody Betty ride had a rusted steel track that ran along the front of the colorfully painted facade. The backdrop above the track rose over their heads at least eight feet. It was painted with garish colors and showed fierce pirates wearing handkerchiefs tied around their heads, brandishing knives, and waving flintlock pistols. She had seen several such pistols in the Weapons of History exhibit at the L.I.P.S. museum, dedicated to the history of the L.I.P.S.

A tall man she'd not seen before appeared from the dark tunnel on the left side of the Bloody Betty ride. His eyes were fixed on the oily cloth he used to wipe his hands. His dirty-blond hair was cut short, as if he were military.

Aloha had met a lot of military types in the course of her job as a spy, and he didn't carry himself like they did, so she assumed he was a normal guy. His denim coveralls and gray work shirt were spotted with smudges of black grease. A black smudge ran across his strong jaw and up his left cheek, where it faded like smoke from a campfire. He looked lean, yet muscular. His biceps bulged. He finally looked up from wiping his hands, and his coffee-colored eyes widened when he saw her and Stinky coming toward him.

Aloha's heartbeat increased, and she wiped the palm of her right hand on her pant leg, hoping no one noticed. The man wasn't hard on the eyes. But she needed to be professional and keep her feelings in check. She didn't need her head turned every time she ran into a handsome man.

Work before pleasure. That was her motto.

Aloha smiled. He offered her a sly smile in return, accentuating a dimple in his right cheek.

Whoa! Aloha fanned herself with her right hand, and her breathing became ragged. Perhaps she was being a little strict with that motto. Maybe there was time for a quick kiss, or a hug. *What would that hurt?*

He broke eye contact with her and glanced toward his boss. "Hey, Mr. O'Lanigan," he said, his brown eyes sparkling in the waning sunlight. It was late afternoon and the shadows had begun to lengthen; the sun would disappear in another hour or so.

"Hi, Pete. You got the Bloody Betty ride working yet?"

Pete glanced away from Stinky toward the Bloody Betty. "Well, I got the generator running, and the gears for the track mechanism aren't frozen anymore. I have three cars on the track now. We can test it any time you like."

Stinky nodded. "Good job, Pete. I'd like to see the cars moving now, please."

Pete looked back at Aloha and offered her a half smile, then turned and headed back into the dark tunnel.

"Oh, Pete," Stinky said, causing Pete to turn back toward them. "This is Aloha Armstrong. She's going to be our new Bloody Betty."

Pete's gaze flitted to Aloha's, then roamed over her face as he studied her. Aloha's heart beat faster under the mechanic's steady, confident eyes.

"Pete, the cars," said Stinky.

Pete looked at his boss, shrugged, and stuffed the oily rag in his back pocket. "Okay, you stay here and watch for the cars coming out of the right side of the tunnel." He pointed at the opening where the track disappeared into darkness.

Pete hurried away, disappearing into the shadows inside the tunnel.

The echo of his footsteps abruptly stopped, followed by the grinding of gears and the metallic squeal of steel on steel.

Aloha winced and covered her ears with her hands. She glanced at Stinky. "What's the ride supposed to do?"

Stinky swiveled his head to look at her, then shouted, "The cars transport riders to the days when cutthroat pirates sailed the Spanish Main."

Aloha nodded and smiled to herself. *This broken-down ride is going to make someone think they're in the days of the buccaneers? Yeah, right.*

No doubt, once inside the ride, patrons would see fake scenes made with cardboard and plywood held together with spit and duct tape. There'd be bad actors pretending to be bloodthirsty pirates. It might scare the kiddies, sure. From the look of this theme park, it was obvious they couldn't afford animatronic pirates, and she, unfortunately, would be the poor substitute.

I'll bet there's not a B.U.T.T.S. agent within a thousand miles of this place. The Director had to be wrong. The intelligence was bad. That had to be it.

The sound of grinding gears and stressed metal continued to echo from the tunnel, followed by a rumble that signaled the cars were finally headed out.

After several seconds, three empty cars appeared. Their exteriors were riddled with strips of peeled paint, and rusted handrails were attached to the rounded nose of each car. A cable linked the cars, and they moved as one along the narrow track. When they reached the middle of the tunnel opening, they stopped as the generator sputtered and the echo died.

There was now silence—and no sign of Pete.

Aloha's finely tuned spy senses niggled at her. A growing sense of unease enveloped her. Something had happened to Pete. She'd fought vampires, zombies, evil geniuses, and monsters of all kinds, but this didn't feel like any of those things. No, something else was going on, something actually worse than monsters.

Stinky must have sensed it, too. "That's odd," he said.

"What?" The small hairs at the nape of her neck rose.

"Where's Pete?" said Stinky.

Aloha's brow wrinkled. If Stinky didn't know where Pete was...

This situation needed more investigation before she hit the panic button. If the B.U.T.T.S. were here, then real trouble could be hiding just under the surface.

"Do you have a flashlight?" she asked.

Stinky looked at her, his eyes quizzical.

"I am supposed to be the marquee character for the ride, right?"

Stinky nodded.

"Okay, so in a way I'm responsible for what happens on the ride, right?"

Stinky shrugged.

I'm stretching my logic again. "Well regardless, I'm going to go look around. See if I can find Pete."

Stinky shrugged again and swept aside his jacket. Hanging off his belt was a yellow-and-black flashlight. He unhooked it, then handed it to her. "Okay, but be careful. The wood flooring has dry rot and Pete could have gotten stuck." He paused and avoided her gaze. "It's not the safest place in there."

"Don't worry," she offered him a smile. "I'll find him."

Gripping her handbag tightly, she ran into the tunnel and snapped on the flashlight as the darkness closed around her.

The track curved to her left and disappeared around a corner. She kept the fierce white shaft of light focused on the rusted steel tracks and followed the curve of the wall.

Her nose wrinkled as the smells of decaying plant material invaded her senses.

There was a chocolate-brown wall straight ahead that ran from the floor of the tunnel to the ceiling. The track ran through the center of the tunnel, and the black walls on either side of the track were unbroken by doors or windows. The wall ahead appeared to be a dead end, and there was no sign of Pete.

"Hey, Pete!" The echo of her words slowly died off. There was no reply. No sound of footsteps other than her own. Not the sound of breathing. Nothing. But her experienced spy senses were tingling.

Aloha frowned. This was all very odd. *Where could he be?*

She scanned the area around her with the flashlight. The light beam revealed the now-silent generator. The faint odor of gas cut through the scent of the aging structure around her.

Aloha walked up to the wall and studied it with narrow eyes. Her curiosity was piqued. Why was this wall brown when the others were all black? It was like one of those locked-room mysteries.

She shook her head. There had to be something behind this wall. There was nowhere else for Pete to go, given there was only one entrance and one exit to the ride, and the missing man had yet to appear at neither. Maybe there was a secret door, but that was so cliché.

In her experience though, the obvious, even a clichéd one, was sometimes the correct answer.

Fortunately, hidden in a false compartment of her handbag, she had the particle scanner provided by Dr. Oh of the L.I.P.S. Research and Development division.

Dr. Oh supplied L.I.P.S field agents with a number of exotic weapons and gadgets, but her favorite was the particle scanner. The device's beam could penetrate any material, revealing secret passageways and enemies hiding behind walls. The gadget had saved her life many times during her most dangerous missions.

Aloha set the flashlight on the top of the generator and pointed the beam of light at the wall. After unzipping her bag, she approached and laid one hand on the wall's surface. It was cool to the touch. Her heart beat harder. Her senses were on high alert. She sensed danger. Reaching into her bag, she pressed the release button in the liner.

There was an audible *click* as she released the latch over the hidden compartment at the bottom of the bag to reveal the particle scanner and two other secret weapons. She pulled out the scanner and then closed and resealed the compartment.

The scanner was about the size of a tube of lipstick. The bottom half was burnished black; the top half was polished stainless steel.

Aloha pointed the device at the wall and then gripped the top in the fingers of her right hand, while with the other hand she twisted the bottom. The device began to hum softly in the confined space, and out of the bottom came a small screen about three inches wide by two inches deep that hinged up so she could see any image on the screen. The screen would feed her information about the results of the scans. It was the Swiss army knife of the L.I.P.S. arsenal.

With the scanner now fully deployed, Aloha again picked up the flashlight from on top of the generator and moved closer to the blank wall, holding the device in front of her.

Raising the scanner to the wall, she began to sweep it back and forth to try to get a reading of what was behind the wall that she hadn't noticed from the outside. The tiny screen showed only ordinary wood until there was a spike in energy. She froze in place and held the scanner steady.

Her brow wrinkled. *Fascinating. I've seen readings like this before. I wish I could remember where.*

It couldn't be the bomb she'd come here to find. The source of the radiation wasn't electrical, or nuclear, or even battery powered. The line on the graph displayed on the tiny screen spiked again, then once again settled to the normal range of background radiation.

She licked her lips and didn't move the scanner. She recalled when she'd seen the readings before. A year back, a case of lycanthropy had taken her to Chernobyl, inside Russia. The radiation she was seeing on the scanner screen matched what she'd seen there. It was coming from a radioactive isotope.

Her heart rate increased. "So not good," she muttered under her breath. This had to be a B.U.T.T.S. death trap, and she'd fallen right into it.

No way was this mission going to be her first failure. She gritted her teeth. *No way.*

Suddenly everything around her was consumed in a blinding white light. Under assault of the bright light, Aloha yelped in pain and closed her eyes. She dropped the scanner as she instinctively covered her eyes with her arms.

She stumbled backward. The room began to spin around her. Her stomach heaved, and she thought she'd vomit when bile rose at the back of her throat.

Finally the spinning sensation eased and she dropped to her knees, wincing when they struck wooden planks. The planks trembled under her the wood rising and falling as if she were on her uncle's yacht. The smell of salty air invaded her nostrils, reminding her of the seashore. And a warm breeze brushed the skin of her bare arms and her cheeks.

She sniffed, and the strong odor of brine invaded her mouth and nose. The moving planks beneath her rolled side to side, and she had to tense to keep from falling on her side. Her heart beat rapidly. She couldn't see, and her surroundings had definitely changed.

She nearly jumped out of her skin when there was the sharp cry of a bird from overhead. Was that a seagull? *Impossible. I must be dreaming.*

Where am I? Slowly she dropped her arms and extended her hands to the planks beneath her. Her fingers brushed over rough, damp wood. Fear gripped her. She sat back on her haunches, her mind whirling with uncertainty. *I hope I didn't set off the bomb. If I did, then it's goodbye, butt.*

She tried opening one eye but was forced to squeeze it shut again due to the unexpectedly bright sunlight.

Her mind raced with confusion. How could there be warm sunlight, when it was going to be dark soon? None of this made any sense to her.

"Cap'n, what be this woman aboard the ship? How did she git here?"

She froze. *Who's that?* He didn't sound friendly, and he didn't sound like Stinky or Pete. She was temporarily blinded, and an unknown, possibly hostile, male was near her. She needed to get out of there, and fast. *Think, girl...*

She swallowed hard as fear invaded her mind. *You've been in worse scrapes than this.*

The clicking sound of a pistol hammer being locked frightened her; she took in a shaky breath.

Uhhh, maybe not worse than this. Now he's going to shoot me? Why? She winced, waiting for the inevitable shot.

"Hold there, Mr. Knight," a familiar voice ordered.

Aloha slowly opened one eye and squinted, but she could make out only indistinct shapes moving around her. She forced the other eye open.

The blurry shapes began to coalesce into the most remarkable men she had ever seen. Her mouth hung open as she scanned the group standing over her.

They were all dressed as pirates, with muscular, bare chests and faces as hard as granite, dotted with ragged scars. They wore baggy pants, and most held cutlasses at the ready.

The pirate standing nearest her on the heaving wooden deck held a museum-quality flintlock pistol aimed directly at her head. His blazing eyes and snarling mouth showed he wasn't happy to have his target practice interrupted. *Good for me, since I'm the target.*

"Mr. Knight. Men. This is Bloody Betty, Queen of the Pirates."

Aloha blinked to further clear her blurred vision and looked at the man speaking. There, standing on the forecastle of the ship, was Pete from the theme park. He wore a billowing white shirt open to the waist, black pants, knee-high leather boots, and his curly blond hair spilled over his shoulders from beneath a wide-brimmed hat with a black feather stuck into the band. Pete's new look was terrific. Her attraction to him had just grown by leaps and bounds.

But why had Pete just called her Bloody Betty, Queen of the Pirates? She shook her head as confusion threatened to overwhelm her. *He can't mean...?* How could this be? Suddenly she realized. *Oh, crap.* Pete wanted her to be the *real* Bloody Betty! *Why?*

A flapping sound coming from overhead made her look up. She squinted as her vision cleared. There, attached to the main mast of the ship, a black flag with the painted image of a white skull and crossbones fluttered in the breeze.

I don't think I'm in Kansas anymore. Or Florida, for that matter. She groaned inwardly. *Time travel. Crap.*

***

Aloha sat across the chart table from Pete, or as he called himself now, Black Pete, scourge of the Spanish Main. If she was here, then perhaps so was the X-Factor bomb. She had to find it, or the past and the future might go up in smoke.

Pete sat in his chair, his back to her, whispering to his first mate, Mr. Knight.

The wooden-hulled ship with its billowing sails, the guns on the wooden deck, the smell of black powder, the clothes the men wore, the flintlocks and sabers in their belts—this coupled with the men's manner of speaking meant she had somehow been transported to the late eighteenth century. Though with Pete's long mane he must have been here longer than her. Too often time travel screwed with you like that.

The tropical heat and sparkling blue of the ocean suggested they were sailing somewhere in the Caribbean Sea, or perhaps the South Pacific. From her recollection of the history taught at the L.I.P.S. academy, this was more likely the former if these were indeed pirates. (And was she really considering this? She supposed she was.) These men spoke with an English accent. Eighteenth-century pirates pillaged British and Spanish ships in the Caribbean, not the South Pacific. Sometimes they acted as privateers or as pawns of the major European powers of the day.

Pete provided her with pirate clothing that felt heavy and thick, yet baggy and loose about her arms and legs. The clothes were at least practical for the pirate profession of the era. *And I look cool in them.*

She'd managed to hang on to her handbag. She'd need her L.I.P.S. weapons if she were to survive. Women on sailing vessels of the period were thought to be bad luck. She might have to fight her way out of a jam unless she played her cards right. For now she'd have to play the part of Bloody Betty, Queen of the Pirates, until she found a way off the ship and a way back to her own time.

She'd been in worse jams than this. Bloodthirsty vampires and werewolves made pirates seem like pussycats. Heavily armed pussycats to be sure, but at least they were human.

Mr. Knight was searching her bag, and when he didn't find anything he would recognize as a weapon, he gave it back to her.

Even if they were found in the secret compartment, a modern villain would have trouble recognizing Dr. Oh's weapons and spy gadgets. Something she'd used to her advantage on more than one occasion.

These two burly, bare-chested pirates with their sinewy arms crossed over their wide chests were a dangerous and bloodthirsty couple of cutthroats.

Not that she was easily frightened of these men.

She was almost six feet tall, with flowing, fiery red hair and dazzling green eyes that pierced them with her best glares. She could keep the motley crew at bay. Of course, the sword in the sheath Pete had given her, now hanging off her wide hip, backed up her striking appearance.

In fact, it made her angry they would even think she was some weak woman. She was a secret agent, who could fight her way of out here if it came to them or her. Aloha didn't fear death, and from the look of these two cutthroats, neither did they. They each wore a thick, black leather belt stuffed with two flintlocks and a dagger. Their dark eyes were watchful, and they scowled at her.

Well, this woman would show them that a twenty-first-century L.I.P.S. woman would knock some heads and take names if need be, to send them the message not to mess with her.

She crossed her legs at the ankles and eased back against the dowels of the chair, laying her arms flat on the armrests. With her L.I.P.S. academy early-threat-detection training, she was capable of dealing with any danger before it came at her.

The wood dowels on the back of the chair were rough as they pressed into her back.

The cabin air was riddled with a myriad of odors. Candle wax, stale rum, and sweat mingled with a hint of spent cooking grease. But there was a trace of something else in the air. Something didn't fit these antique surroundings.

Sitting up in the chair, she tensed. She sniffed the air. *Was that machine oil?* Her heart beat faster, and her eyes narrowed when she recognized the smell.

Something from the twenty-first century had to be nearby. Nothing from this period used machine oil. She considered what it might be.

Pete was here. She was here. Her heart skipped a beat. The bomb she'd been looking for back at the amusement park...

Her mission wasn't a failure, after all. The X-Factor bomb had to be here somewhere, but where?

There was no point in fumbling around in the dark. If the X-Factor bomb had been transported to this time, then it might go off before she could defuse it. She had to find it.

But first she had to find out if Pete was a B.U.T.T.S. agent and if he knew where the bomb was located. She decided to befriend him. Of course, it was certainly easier when he had saved her life a few times. And he was a handsome stud muffin.

Good thing she'd done well in the advanced bomb diffusion course she had taken at the L.I.P.S. academy. She enjoyed diffusing bombs and had deactivated several in her career.

Professor A.L. Thumbs will be so proud of his number-one student when I save the world. Again.

She leaned forward and craned her neck so she could see the maps on the chart table. One map in particular intrigued her because it had an outline of an island in the middle of an empty section of ocean. *I suspect that island's off the normal trade routes*, she mused. *But why would he be interested in a remote island with no rich targets for plundering or pirating or whatever pirates do?*

Pete finally finished his conversation with Knight. He looked to her. Gazing into her eyes, his lips formed a sly smile and his eyes sparkled.

She wished she knew more about what was going on here. She needed information if she was to survive in this time period.

"Where am I?" she said haughtily. Aloha suspected where she was, but she needed the facts and nothing but the facts.

The first mate looked up from the map he'd been studying to glare at her. He moved slowly around the table.

Aloha's gaze held his; she hoped she projected all the anger and defiance flowing through her. Her lean frame tensed, and her hands formed fists.

"No woman talks ta me cap'n like that," Knight growled as he stepped forward. He withdrew his dagger from his belt; the razor-sharp blade glinted in the candlelight. He took a step closer, still raising the blade, looking ready to slit her throat.

Aloha didn't move. She set her jaw, her gaze hard as diamonds as she stared down the first mate, silently daring him to take a swing at her. She would drop the man on his ass if he tried anything with that knife.

Pete chuckled. "Now, now, Mr. Knight, let's not be too hasty."

Knight hesitated and looked to Pete. "But, cap'n, she's been speakin' disrespectful ta you. No whore speaks ta you like she does and lives."

Pete chuckled again. "Oh, I assure you, Mr. Knight, this woman is no whore. She's as deadly a pirate wench as these waters have ever seen."

"You bet your sweet butt, bucko," Aloha said scornfully, while arching an eyebrow at Knight.

The first mate's dirt-streaked features turned a deep shade of scarlet.

Aloha kept her gaze on Knight. "Why, I ought a kill you where you stand," she added for good measure.

Knight's knuckles turned white, and he ground his teeth. The sound reminded Aloha of fingernails on a chalkboard. There was definitely murder in his eyes. No matter. She had faced far bigger and far more deadly men than this.

She had to try not to kill Knight; if she could avoid it, she would. His descendants might be important to the future. If she killed him now, then she might create a paradox.

No, she decided, it would be best to knock him out if he attacked her.

She glanced at Pete. His six-pack abs were visible in the opening of his shirt. His wide mouth formed a lopsided grin, and his blond curly hair draped over his broad shoulders.

Pete sure seems to be relishing his role. He's fitting in better than I am. She eyed the pirate captain, still seated in his chair watching her.

Pete was somehow more attractive in the past than he was in the future. Maybe it was the rough pirate look.

Aloha swallowed. But she had never let a pretty face get in the way of her mission—especially when the mission had been thrown a time-travel curveball.

If the X-Factor bomb went off in the past, the future could be destroyed—and she couldn't let that happen. No, she had to stay focused.

Knight moved a step closer, his thin, cruel mouth forming a grim line and his eyes flaring. Aloha held her ground and prepared for his attack. Her heart beat quickened and she controlled her breathing; her stomach muscles tightened. The first mate kept his knife lowered. His eyes flitted to Pete, who sat watchful but silent, then back to her.

What is he waiting for? she wondered.

Pete waved at Knight to back away. Knight growled but did as he was told, sheathing his knife once again in the scabbard on his belt. Pete's eyes flitted to Aloha. "I like your spirit, Betty. You don't back down from any man." He glanced at his first mate. Knight's cheeks flushed crimson.

Thanks a lot, Pete. Now your guy really hates me.

"Mr. Knight, go topside and make sure the lookouts are alert and ready to report anything out of the ordinary." Pete waved a dismissive hand at the guards on either side of the cabin door. "And take those two with you."

Knight's features sagged.

He opened his mouth to protest, but obviously thought better of it and snapped his mouth shut before stuffing his dagger into the sheath on his belt.

"Com'on, lads," he said gruffly to the two guards.

The cabin door slammed shut behind them, leaving Aloha and Pete alone for the first time since she'd come aboard.

"Well, what do you think, Miss Armstrong? Sweet set up, don't you think?"

Aloha smiled. "Yes, I agree, Pete." She stood and paced in front of the chart table. She could sense his eyes following her, but she avoided his gaze. "I've been trying to figure out why you kept me from getting my throat slit. It occurred to me there are two possibilities." She stopped pacing and turned to face him.

"One: you love me."

He grinned.

She shook her head. "Ridiculous, of course. We just met." He opened his mouth to speak, but she waved him away.

Pete gazed at her, his eyes twinkling and a sly smile on his lips.

Aloha waved a hand at him. "I don't buy that love-at-first-sight BS."

She turned away and walked to the window looking out over the stern of the ship at the rolling sea beyond. She continued, "Two: I believe you work for B.U.T.T.S., which means you and I are enemies. Regardless, you need me. I don't know for what, but I'm grateful, no matter what the reason." She turned to face him once again.

The smile faded from Pete's sunbaked features. "How do you know I work for B.U.T.T.S.?" He paused, and his eyes flitted side to side. "I mean—what's B.U.T.T.S.? I mean, besides the obvious?"

Aloha chuckled and moved to the chair across the table from Pete. "As you well know, the L.I.P.S. have been all over the B.U.T.T.S. for over three hundred years. We L.I.P.S. agents can always smell out an enemy agent." Her nose wrinkled. "And this B.U.T.T.S. agent smells fishy to me."

Pete winced. "That obvious, huh?"

Aloha shrugged.

"Okay. Yes, I'm a B.U.T.T.S. agent, and you're right, I do need your help. Desperately." He shook his head. "But I didn't realize there was another B.U.T.T.S. agent from the future already among the crew." His voice had a bitter edge to it. "If that agent gets his hands on the X-Factor bomb, he plans to detonate it.

He had secret orders I wasn't privy to. Apparently, he's supposed to detonate the bomb to create an alternate future where the B.U.T.T.S. rule the world. The big bosses didn't trust me to complete the mission. I'm a decoy to distract any L.I.P.S. agents that came after the bomb. So, you see, I'm expendable."

Expendable? Sad when your employer thinks so little of you. Then again, B.U.T.T.S. is an evil organization. You take your chances when you work for the bad guys.

Aloha eyed the handsome enemy agent dressed like Johnny Depp. "Okay, Pete. No problemo. Let's find this other agent, then we'll talk. Agreed?"

He nodded, but not as enthusiastically as she'd hoped.

His eyes narrowed, and he avoided her gaze.

Her trouble senses were acting up again. Pete wasn't telling her something. Something serious. Then a thought occurred to her. "Tell me you still have the X-Factor bomb." *Please say yes. Please say yes. Please say yes.*

He shook his head.

Great, she thought, *I finally meet a nice enemy agent needing my help who I could have been friends with—instead we're going to blow up together in the past.*

Why does this kind of stuff always happen to me?

"So who is this other B.U.T.T.S. agent?"

Pete sighed. "I've been working on that. I've narrowed it down to the cook and Mr. Knight. When I arrived in Tortuga six months ago—"

"Six months ago?"

Pete nodded. "As far as I can tell when we—by this I mean you and me—traveled in time to the eighteenth century..." He paused to gather his thoughts. "...We arrived six months apart."

Aloha nodded. Time travel was far from an exact science.

"Anyway," Pete continued, "I was shanghaied in Tortuga and brought aboard this ship, the *Satan's Revenge*. Since I'm a trained fencer, I proved quite valuable to the previous captain—"

"Previous captain?" Aloha arched an eyebrow.

"The previous captain was killed in a battle, so I *assumed* command."

The way he said assumed made Aloha think he probably kicked some asses and took some names. *Nice. I like tough guys.* Aloha smiled thinly. "But how? These cutthroats would happily slice you into little pieces and feed your bits to the sharks."

"I told them I knew the location of the richest treasure in the world."

She grinned. "That would work. Nice job." She stood and leaned across the map table. The palms of her hands now lay flat on the rough wood. *I preferred my version, but if it works, why not?*

She gazed into his eyes, and her heart began to beat faster. *I think I'm falling for this guy.* She didn't want to, but she couldn't help herself. Pete had saved her life. He was her kind of man. And he was sexy, which certainly didn't hurt.

She cleared her throat. "Then there's the matter of the X-Factor bomb." She turned away to scan the room. "Do you know where it is?"

"Huh, when I realized my boss was going to liquidate me, I was seriously pissed off, so I threw it overboard."

Spies loved to use words like liquidate. It meant to kill someone, but it seemed better to soften the wording, though in the case of the X-Factor bomb, 'liquidate' was pretty much dead-on.

Aloha's brow wrinkled. Her spy senses were tingling again. The uncertain edge she detected in Pete's tone of voice suggested he was lying, but why? Aloha frowned, her stomach knotted with anger, and her mouth dried. The future was at stake, and she had to find the bomb, defuse it, and find a way home.

Preferably in that order, or the future she so loved would be gone forever. The world would be under control of one big B.U.T.T.S.

Aloha turned back to Pete and picked up the map with the hand-drawn island in the center of an empty ocean. Hand-drawn? Something was wrong. Were they headed to the right place? "The bomb is on this island, isn't it? It got buried there." She pointed to the black X painted on one end of the roughly drawn, kidney-shaped island. "And you have no idea how to get there, do you?"

Pete lifted his gaze and grinned. "Nothing gets past you, does it?"

Aloha smirked. "No," she said flatly. "But Knight saw the map. He also knows how to find the island, correct? This means Knight and the late captain knew the exact location of the island."

Pete grinned. "Just as you say, Miss Armstrong."

Aloha looked up from the map and smiled. "You may call me Aloha. There's also a buried treasure. Correct?"

Pete's eyes narrowed, and his smile disappeared. He moved around the table and now stood next to her. She loved the masculine way he carried himself and the earthy scent of him. *Keep your mind on your work, girl.*

"Yes," his voice was deep and earnest. "But before the power cell in my particle scanner died, I detected a powerful energy source in the direction of this general area." He took a pencil and marked the ship's current position, then drew a line east, ending dead center on the island, "at these coordinates on the map. This confirms we're headed to the right place."

"What was this energy source?"

He shook his head. " I don't know. But I believe that near the treasure on that island is a source of energy that will open a time portal." He paused and looked at her. "A way home."

"Really? Is it that powerful?"

"Yes, it's more powerful than ten hydrogen bombs. Unimaginable power that will make whoever possesses it master of the world. You can imagine what will happen if it gets into the wrong hands."

Aloha grew cold as the realization of what he was saying took hold. A knot of excitement formed in the pit of her stomach. A way home? *We have to find that energy source, whatever it is.*

He stood straight and sighed. "But I don't know exactly where the treasure is. The captain and Mr. Knight buried it alone." He looked at her and smiled.

Her excitement faded. "How long until we arrive at the island?" she asked.

"I'm not sure. We've been under sail for two days and headed in the right direction, but the map doesn't have exact coordinates—"

A heavy pounding on the cabin door interrupted them. "What is it?" Pete shouted.

"Cap'n, the lookouts report they've spotted a ship off the larboard side, headed for us. And there's an island dead ahead, sir."

Pete looked at Aloha, his eyes wide.

"Well, that was fast," she said. Her body tensed. The knot of excitement returned. *This is sooo cool. It's like being in a real pirate story.* She hesitated. *This is a real pirate story. And we could be home soon.*

The energy source in that treasure had to be something very important. But what could it be?

Pete walked across the room to a wardrobe and swung the door open; the hinges squealed loudly. He pulled out two cutlasses, slid into basket guards.

Drawing her own sword, she blew out a breath. *I'm a spy, not a musketeer.*

She shrugged. *Oh well, when in the Caribbean...* She hefted the sword to test its weight. It was heavier than she would have imagined, but the cool steel of the hilt felt good against her skin. She withdrew the cutlass from the guard and studied the blade. And the blade certainly looked sharp enough.

Problem was, she had never been good with swords. A .45 automatic, a 50 caliber a machine gun, even a few throwing stars—sure, those she knew how to use, but a sword?

Her eyes narrowed, and she became excited. *A good, old-fashioned sword fight might be fun*, she thought. She'd always relished a challenge.

"Com'on," Pete said, his voice urgent.

Aloha offered him a tight smile. "Are we under attack?" she asked as she followed him to the cabin door.

"Yup. You're going to have to prove you're the real Bloody Betty," he said grimly.

They exited the cabin together, only to be struck in the face by the salty sea breeze. A dull thump of cannon fire rent the air.

Aloha and Pete moved to the side of the ship, looking over an expanse of ocean at a much larger ship. Its billowing white sails were fully extended by the strong wind, and it sliced through the sea. White foam sprayed both sides of the hull as it quickly closed the distance between them.

Aloha swallowed hard. *I may have bit off a little more than I can chew*. Her eyes flitted to the cutlass in her hand. She gripped the handle tighter as her palms began to sweat.

The ship coming at them had two large masts, and it had a second deck above the water line, bristling with gun ports.

Attached to the top of the other ship's main mast flew a skull-and-crossbones flag, snapping in the wind. The massive enemy ship was another pirate ship. *And pirates are cutthroats*, she reminded herself.

Her lips dried. Fear gripped her, and her hands trembled. *We will have to fight, or we will die.* The pirates on both ships were far better with swords than she was, and the other ship had far more guns than she'd seen on the *Satan's Revenge*.

"Do we have any chance of beating them?" she whispered.

Pete turned to look at her. His eyes drooped, and he shook his head. "None. Zero. Unless you have something magical in your handbag."

The corners of Aloha's mouth curled up. "As a matter of fact, I might have just the thing the doctor ordered."

***

Dr. Oh's sonic thrower cut the enemy ship in two within seconds. It was as easy as slicing pie.

There were no flames, just a clean cut that sliced the ship in half from bow to stern. Both halves fell over and quickly slipped beneath the waves. What remained of the enemy crew splashed in the sea, scattered across the foam trail left by the two halves of the hull. Bits of wood and shattered barrels dotted the surface of the water. Some of the men had managed to grab on to the flotsam as if it were buoys.

Good thing that Dr. Oh had included the weapon in her gear. Though to most people it looked like eyeliner, the sonic thrower emitted a sonic scream along a narrow beam that could cut through steel.

Aloha turned away from the wreckage of the enemy ship and the crew floundering in the ocean to find the crew of the *Satan's Revenge* cowering, their eyes wide with fear. As if they were glued together, they slowly backed away from her. Several gripped the crosses hung on strings around their necks while their lips moved in silent prayer.

As she recalled, witches were burned at the stake in this period of history. She may have just sealed her fate by saving them. *Great.* Talk about irony.

She glanced at Pete, hoping he would once again save her from certain doom. As if he'd read her mind, Pete was all smiles. "Sweet! Nice work, Betty."

She grinned at him and her cheeks grew warm. She was acting like a schoolgirl, in love for the first time. *Get a grip, girl.*

"They seem to be able to swim," she pointed at the enemy crew struggling in the sea. Her heart froze when one man slipped beneath the water. Just before he disappeared, his mouth opened as if to scream, but the sound was lost as he went under.

She looked back at Pete, who shook his head. "Sorry, most sailors in this period don't know how to swim."

Aloha's eyes went wide with horror. She couldn't believe what she'd just done. It wasn't like she'd wanted to, but she'd just killed an entire ship's crew with one shot.

"*What was that,* cap'n?"

Aloha started at the sound of the angry voice of the first mate, coming from behind them.

Pete and Aloha turned around to find Knight aiming two fully loaded and cocked flintlocks at them.

"Mr. Knight." Pete scowled at his crewman. "What's the meaning of this?"

The first mate's slash of a mouth formed a lopsided smile. It was more a grimace than a smile, but because his face was so scarred and sun-weathered, it seemed the best he could manage.

"As you said yerself, cap'n, you and this witch aren't from these parts. We have no need for da cursed on this ship." He tilted his head to indicate something off the port bow, where there was a cloud bank beginning to clear.

Aloha's eyes followed the line of sight suggested by Knight. Her jaw dropped as the cloud cover at last lifted.

There was an island. A green, heavily forested island, with a towering volcano sticking from the center of thick stands of palm trees. The peak of the volcano trailed ink-black smoke. It had to be the island on the map.

"There is the island with the treasure, the one on the map."

Aloha's stomach tightened when she realized she'd been correct. Knight would lead them to the treasure, and the mysterious energy source. This might be their chance to get home.

"And it be the place you and the missus will be callin' home from this day forward," the first mate added.

Aloha glanced at Pete and grimaced. He didn't look happy, yet they both knew if they wanted to get home, they had to appear to be playing along. Pete tipped his chin slightly, indicating he understood. *Great.*

Now they were really on the losing end of this mess.

Knight glanced over his shoulder with the flintlocks still aimed at their chests. He looked back at them with an evil grin on his weathered features.

"Isn't that right, mates?" Knight shouted.

There were roars of approval with scattered calls of, "Aye, aye, Cap'n Knight!" from the assembled crew on the deck.

Oh, crap. If Knight was the B.U.T.T.S. agent as Pete suspected, then he was going to get hold of the treasure and the bomb, and they'd lose their chance to control the mysterious energy Pete's scanner had detected. And if that happened, whatever the new energy was would be controlled by B.U.T.T.S., not L.I.P.S. This was bad. Her job was to ensure good always won. She had to find the treasure, stop B.U.T.T.S., and save the world. Again.

She had never felt so frustrated. This mission had gone sideways.

I have to do something. Her stomach muscles tightened. She really wanted to wipe the deck with this puke. *He's a mutineer!*

But for now they'd bide their time and wait for the right opportunity to turn the tables in their favor.

Her eyes flitted to Pete and she saw his jawline tighten and his eyes become hard. *Of course, Pete might strangle the bastard first.*

Knight ordered one of his crew to take their weapons, including the sonic thrower, which was immediately thrown overboard.

Great. Superstitious fools just threw away millions spent on research and development to make the thing. A knot of anger rose in her belly. She detested waste.

"Tie them up in the galley, men."

Two burly sailors grabbed Aloha by her arms and held her. She glared at each man in turn and considered ripping them apart, or going all postal on their butts. For now she'd wait. She'd wait until they really pissed her off. She suspected that wouldn't take long.

Regardless, when she got out of this mess, she'd kick their asses with a few judo moves.

Two other sailors grabbed Pete by his arms and tossed him to the deck, where he landed facedown with a *smack*.

Now she had double the reason to teach these bastards a lesson. Her stomach muscles tightened and her hands formed fists. Her heart rate increased. No one beat up her friends. No one.

Knight raised his pistols into the air and fired them simultaneously.

"Mates, we're about to become richer than the bleeding King of England!"

***

When all but two of the crew left the ship for the island, Knight told them once he and the crew returned she and Pete would be shark food.

Aloha managed to untie the ropes holding her hands. The rope-tying—and un-tying—skills she learned when she was a Girl Scout sure came in handy today. They escaped from the galley and the remaining crew by using the compact-shaped invisibility generator provided by Dr. Oh. It was only good for a one-time use because it sucked up so much power, but thirty-two minutes was sufficient time for them to slip over the side and swim to shore. Good thing the unit was waterproof.

Dr. Oh thinks of everything, Aloha mused.

Aloha now stood with her back to a palm tree, her breath coming in gasps. Running in this heat and humidity drained a person's energy very quickly.

Pete leaned against the other side of the tree and was also breathing hard. She and Pete were partners for the rest of the mission.

And maybe once they were home they could go for a drink or catch a movie—if they made it back.

The island's air was thick with humidity, and biting insects buzzed about them. But, oddly, there were no bird or other animal sounds.

There was a large stand of palm trees in front of them, the trunks overgrown by ferns and bushes. The echo of a gruff voice shouting orders came from the direction of the trees. Aloha looked at Pete, pointed to the bushes, and silently mouthed that Knight and the pirates were on the other side. Pete nodded.

They had to capture Knight and make him reveal the location of the treasure, and hopefully the bomb. Aloha hoped the bomb was with the treasure. In fact, she was counting on it.

Moving as quietly as possible, Aloha stepped through the trees and soon stepped onto the beach, followed by Pete. The pirate crew stood facing them, but Knight had his back to them.

Upon seeing Aloha and Pete suddenly appear as if from thin air when the invisibility generator's power cell was drained, the crew scattered, running into the forest yelling, "Witches!" and "God save us!"

"Come back, ya scurvy dogs!" Knight shouted after them, waving his arms in the air above his head. "There's no such thing as witches!"

"I wouldn't be so sure about that," said Aloha.

Knight spun round to face her, a flintlock pistol in his right hand and his cutlass in his left. *This guy must sleep with his weapons.*

Before the mutineer could fire, Pete, standing to Knight's left, stepped forward and struck him across the jaw with his fist. The pirate staggered backward, his flintlock dropping to his side, but he managed to maintain his grip on the pistol butt.

Knight shook his head, then glowered at his attacker. He then leveled the pistol at Pete. Aloha froze and looked between the two men. She couldn't let this happen. Her heart pounded in her ears, and her body shook with anger. If Knight shot Pete, she wouldn't be responsible for her actions.

"Is the crystal with the treasure?" asked Pete.

Knight's eyes narrowed. "Yes, but no way are you getting it. No one is." Knight's accent had disappeared, and with it his disguise as a pirate. Aloha saw him for what he really was: an enemy agent.

"If I can't have the treasure and the way outta here, then neither will you two," growled the B.U.T.T.S. agent.

Aloha's opportunity to attack had opened up. She reacted as quickly as possible, running toward Knight.

She kicked him, striking his right temple hard with the heel of her boot.

Without emitting a sound, the pirate's eyes closed, then he dropped his weapons to the forest floor and collapsed like a puppet whose strings had been cut. Pete moved to the fallen man and rifled his pockets. With a grunt of satisfaction, he pulled out a folded document that had to be the treasure map.

Aloha knelt on the other side of Knight and gripped his wrist. After searching for a pulse for a second or two, she shook her head as she realized the blow had killed him. Aloha looked at Pete and he nodded grimly. Delivering death was all part of the job, something they both knew.

Suddenly the ground began to shake, then shifted violently beneath them, knocking them to the ground.

"Hey! What's happening?" said Aloha.

Aloha covered her head with her arms as stands of palm trees fell like dominoes all around them, and shock waves traveled through her body as she lay on the ground. Fear gripped her. Her heart beat rapidly, and the sour taste of bile came up from the back of her throat.

She removed her hands from her face as the trees stopped falling, to see a large, oil-black cloud tinged with red and orange flames blotting out the sun and the sky. The volcano must have erupted. *We have to get out of here.*

Pete and Aloha struggled to their feet. "What now?" asked Aloha, her breath coming in gasps. Of course, all she wanted was to get the heck out of there, but the mission wasn't over. Volcano or no volcano, she had work to do.

Pete held out the map, scanned it, and then pointed to his right. "We go that way. We have to find the treasure and the bomb, of course. And, I hope, the source of that mysterious energy."

"You're right. But why the treasure? We have to find the bomb and a way out of here, or we'll be toast. And I'm not kidding."

She pointed to the cloud of hot ash that was starting to fill the sky.

Pete explained, "The treasure includes a crystal that will take us back to our time."

Her eyes narrowed. "How do you know?"

"Knight was the B.U.T.T.S. agent I told you about." He looked away, his cheeks crimson.

"I assumed the mysterious energy reading was the crystal. Knight just now confirmed that the crystal is with the treasure."

Aloha considered calling him a nut bar, but in her line of work, she'd seen more than her share of strange stuff. And since she'd already time traveled to an eighteenth-century pirate ship, why couldn't there be magic time-travel crystals?

She rested one hand on his arm. He looked at her. "How did you know Knight was the B.U.T.T.S. agent?"

"Sorry, but I didn't know if I could trust you. Knight told me he would help me find the treasure so we both could go home before he set off the bomb." He paused. 'Then he betrayed me and threatened to kill me."

He had a point. She couldn't blame him for not trusting her. Double agents were far too common in her line of work. So far, Pete had saved her life, and he'd been more of an ally than an enemy.

If she were going to ask him for a date, then it would be better for all concerned if he weren't a B.U.T.T.S. agent. She needed Pete to switch sides. Mixed spy relationships rarely worked. Besides, she had really grown fond of him, and he seemed to like her, as well. Plus, he was really hot. But first things first.

"Okay," she said. "Let's go find that treasure."

***

After they'd been walking for what seemed like forever, they at last came to a cave where Pete said the treasure was hidden. The cave was in the side of a hill, and from there they could see the bay where *Satan's Revenge* was anchored.

Large boulders partially blocked the entrance of the cave. The earthquake must have caused the damage.

"Do you think we can get in?" Aloha asked.

Pete's eyes narrowed. "It's going to be a tight fit, and the cave may fully collapse on top of us if there is another violent earthquake, but I think it's worth the risk."

Aloha wasn't so sure. The rock looked unstable. At that moment some small stones broke free from the top of the cave mouth, snapping over the boulders as they showered the ground.

Aloha had opened her mouth to suggest they forget the whole thing when the volcano in the distance rumbled and spat fiery ashes high, blotting out the blue sky. They were running out of time.

They had to get out of here now. Pete had better be right about those crystals, or their asses were toast.

Aloha followed Pete, who quickly squeezed into the cave entrance.

Aloha crawled on her belly, trying to move as quickly as possible away from the entrance and the flaming ash raining down outside. The temperature had already risen, and Aloha's lungs were burning as she dragged in the hot air. They weren't going to survive very long if they didn't move fast.

She blinked away the sweat that was running into her eyes. "I guess we have no choice now but to find the treasure and hope the story of the crystal is true."

"Oh, it's true." Pete rolled onto his back and took out a pack of matches from his pants pocket. He lit one.

There was enough room for them to stand upright. The cave walls were damp and smelled of must and mold.

Aloha stood and began to brush off her pants. Pete stood as well. He suddenly blew out the match.

"Hey," she protested, "We need *some* light, you know."

Pete pointed ahead of them, farther into the cave. There was a golden glow, brighter than a burning match.

The ground trembled and they were forced to cover their heads with their arms as the cave walls started to give way. "I think we better find that crystal, pronto, and get the heck outta here," said Pete. They ran toward the glow.

They raced around a bend in the tunnel and were stopped short by the glow of the light.

There was a four-foot-high heap of gold coins, ruby- and sapphire-encrusted bracelets, necklaces, and piles of rubies, diamonds, and emeralds in a bowl-shaped, hollowed-out section of rock in the floor of the cave. Set on a peak of brilliant green emeralds was a glowing yellow crystal that sparkled brightly.

The X-Factor bomb lay on the ground next to the pit. It was shaped like a large diamond and perched on one pointed end.

Pete rushed forward. Seizing the bomb, he tucked it under one arm.

Aloha snatched the crystal, then grabbed Pete by his other arm. The air was hotter now and breathing became more difficult with each passing second. The cave began to spin around her, and her vision blurred. If she didn't do something fast, they were done for.

Must think. She stared at the crystal. How does it work? It occurred to her that if a trick worked for Dorothy in the Land of Oz, why not here? It was worth a shot.

Between dry lips Aloha whispered, "There's no place like home. There's no place like home. There's no place like home."

Then she squeezed her eyes tightly closed, and in her mind pictured the Caribbean Islands Holiday Theme Park and Mr. O'Lanigan.

She cried out as a bright white light forced her to shield her eyes with her arms. Immediately the stifling heat disappeared. She took in gulps of cool air. The brush of Pete's arm against hers told her he was still with her. Good.

***

After the light diminished, Aloha blinked to clear her vision. As her sight returned, she was pleased to see Pete's was beside her. They were back at the theme park. They were back in their own time.

A twinge of pain at her right temple made her wince and raise her fingers to her head. Her sudden headache reminded her of the worst hangover ever in her college days. *How I hate time travel.*

But at least the crystal had worked. Sure enough, around her feet were bits of shattered crystal. Apparently, crystallized time travel was a one-way trip. *I'll stick to planes, trains, and automobiles from now on, thank you very much.*

The theme park appeared even more dilapidated than it had when she first arrived.

The Ferris wheel had fallen over, and the other rides had collapsed into heaps of rusted steel. *Hmmm...I hope this is our time.*

Pete accompanied her. Together they walked the grounds calling out, but the only person they found was a caretaker. He was a round man who looked like Santa Claus and said his name was Mr. Whipple.

He said he'd never heard of a Mr. O'Lanigan and explained the theme park had been closed for over twenty years.

No matter how hard you tried, time travel created problems, and history changed. In this case, a paradox had been created. Maybe O'Lanigan had been a descendant of someone on one of the ships, or maybe even Mr. Knight's offspring he may have created in the past. Who knows where he'd been in time and what he'd done to pollute the timeline. B.U.T.T.S. agents were notorious polluters.

If O'Lanigan was his children's ancestor, when they were killed in the past, it erased any future descendants. If it was Knight, it wasn't such a bad outcome, but people being erased from history clearly demonstrated how dangerous time travel could be.

The question remained, though: where and from what era had Knight come from? He might be from her time but he could be from the future.

Aloha doubted she'd ever know the answer to this question, but it'd make an interesting item in her report to the Director.

"So, what about *us?*" asked Pete.

Aloha cast him a sly smile. "If you defected to the L.I.P.S. then I was thinking we should kick the tires and try dating. You game?"

Pete smiled. "After all we've been through, I don't see how we can't."

Aloha laughed. "Yeah. For sure." She arched an eyebrow and nodded to the X-Factor bomb still tucked under Pete's arm. "But we get that thing defused first."

Pete nodded. "Yeah. I think you're right. Maybe we should do that at L.I.P.S. HQ?"

Aloha shrugged. He was right, of course. "Sure, why not?"

Dating an ex-B.U.T.T.S. agent was going to be... different, but maybe she could convince him to join the L.I.P.S. permanently. After all, B.U.T.T.S. had designated him expendable. And stranger things had happened.

Approaching him, she looked deep into his eyes as he wrapped his arms around her and drew her closer. He then kissed her softly on the lips, sending a shiver up her spine. She pressed her lips harder against his and pressed her chest into his.

Her heart thudded against her ribs. She had the feeling that defecting-enemy-agent sex was going to be good, very good.

Her instructors at the academy never told her it would be like this.

Oh, boy, she thought, *that's the understatement of this or any other century.*

About the Author

International selling author, Russ Crossley, writes science fiction and fantasy, and mystery/suspense as well as their various subgenres.

His latest science fiction satire set in the far future, Revenge of the Lushites, is a sequel to Attack of the Lushites released in 2011. The latest title in the series was released in the fall of 2013. Both titles are available in e-book and trade paperback.

He has sold several short stories that have appeared in anthologies from various publishers including; WMG Publishing, Pocket Books, 53rd Street Publishing, and St. Martins Press.

He is a member of SF Canada and is past president of the Greater Vancouver Chapter of Romance Writers of America. He is also an alumni of the Oregon Coast Professional Fiction Writers Master Class taught by award winning author/editors, Kristine Katherine Rusch and Dean Wesley Smith.

Feel free to contact him on Facebook, Twitter, or his website http//:www.russcrossley.com. He loves to hear from readers.

Other titles by Russ Crossley you may enjoy

Razor and Edge Mysteries
The Kidnapping of Billy Buttons
String of Pearls
Death by Clown
Beggin' For Murder
Ragged Ice
The Grand Central Mystery
A Strange Case of Undead Murder

Jazz Stiletto Mysteries
A Day Without Sunshine
Skullduggery
Instrument of justice (first published in Over My Dead Body online mystery magazine)

The Amanda Dark paranormal mysteries
Hook Island
Grind Manor
Moonrise Diner
A Father's Daughter

The Trudy Wilson Mystery Novel Series
Bad Loyalty
Shear Murder
Buzzcut - coming soon

Other Novels

Attack of the Lushites

Revenge of the Lushites
My Zombie Prince
Antique Virgin
The Fire In Their Hearts
with R.S. Meger (from Champagne Books)
Zomopolis
The Last Serial Killer

Short Stories
Countdown
Shoeless Moe
Round Up At The Burger Bar:
The Story of Trixie Pug, Parts 1, 2, 3, 4, 5, 6, 7, 8, 9
Five Minutes
Blossom Queen, Barbarian
The Secret
The Family Line
End of the Flies
Death by Magic
The Penguin Sleeps With The Fishes
Only The Worthy
Hero For A Day
End of Empire
Strange Bedfellows
Big Business
A Perfect Crime
The Wise Guy and The Pirates
In Search of the Perfect Cup
T.I.N. Men
The Legend of G and the Dragonettes
The Incredible Mr. Fix-It
Lock Stock and Barrel

Divided Loyalties
Cave of Wonders
A Family Empire
Until We Meet Again
Dragon Rising
Solitary Man
The Keel Mountain Conspiracy
Angel on My Shoulder
Heroes of Old
The Great Bicycle Race
Tikka's Big Day
"My Partner the Zombie" —
Hungry For Your Love Anthology
(St. Martin's Press)
Big Hairy Deal
One Red Shoe
A Bad Day in Lunden Texas
Bloody Betty, Queen of the Pirates
Mirror Image
Dangerous Waters
Cape Disappointment
Boomerang
The Watcher of Wayburn Street
The Apprentice
Drip!
A Beautiful Friendship and The Parrot of Doom
Robine's Diary
The Christmas Club
Loose Ends
Splatter Pattern
It Takes Two
Lexicon

Replacement Parts
Sidekicks
Lost Stories
Time and Space
Survivors
Neighborhood Watch
Unnatural Immortal
Rum Runner's Lounge
It's A Small Galaxy
A Shattered Man
Betrayed
Replacement Parts
Clubhouse Heroes
Sounds That Angels Make
Muggins Rules – originally published in Fiction River
Volume 12, Risk Takers

Anthologies
Tales of Urban Fantasy
Five Tales of Bizarre Detectives
Tales of Mystery and Suspense
Tales of Weird Fantasy
Tales of Twisted Crime
Tales of The Unexpected
Tales From Space
10 by Russ Crossley
Round Up At The Burger Bar: The Story of Trixie
Pug,
Parts 1- 5 The Beginning
Worlds of Science Fiction and Fantasy
More Tales of Mystery and Suspense
Justice Served

Love Stories
Ladies of the Jolly Roger with Rita Schulz
The Adventures of Razor and Edge:
Five Tales From The Quirky Detective Team
An Unexpected Journey
On Edge
Thrilling Adventures
Total War
Courageous

Non-Fiction

The Writers Tools - The Synopsis

A collection of fifteen stories of wonder and adventure from horror to science fiction to fantasy.

Tales populated with unusual aliens and desperate humans trying to save our future or repair our past. Stories of ghosts, vampires, demons, super heroes and gifted meta humans all trying to save our world.

Angels, hidden worlds, ghosts, star ships orbiting distant planets, a race in a steam punk world to decide the future of an empire. Adventures spanning the galaxy and alternate realities.

Readers will be thrilled by these stories of wonder and adventure.